PUSHPITA
AWASTHI

KNOT OF
Love

SHORT STORIES

novum pro

This book is also
available as
e-book.

www.novum-publishing.co.uk

© 2024 novum publishing

ISBN 978-3-99146-524-9
Editing: Charlotte Middleton
Cover photos: Pushpita Awasthi, Photojogtom | Dreamstime.com
Cover design, layout & typesetting: novum publishing

www.novum-publishing.co.uk

Print product with financial
climate contribution
ClimatePartner.com/16547-2311-1001

Contents

THE KEY

All the town's buses had been painted yellow so that they could enter and move easily in the traffic-controlled areas without any restrictions. This made it difficult for the daily passengers who travelled by bus to recognise their buses. The eyes of unemployed roadside Romeos and street vendors selling their wares (foot-pathiya), gazing up at the young college girls on the school buses, used to be happy and they used to stare at them till the buses passed, but now all the buses were the same. Kishan used to watch this game of sadness and excitement daily while he waited for his routine bus or tempo (3-wheeler).

However fast you move, or run, time always passes in front of your eyes. Kishan remembered a proverb from his childhood – keeping his head at his father's feet when he was laying on his cot, his father, looking at the stars, said that hair is always ahead of time. Son! Know. Kishan believed that in spite of his father's instructions he could not hold the hair of time. And father had been taken away by time. He himself had gone.

The heat of the sun causes the seed to germinate and produce a tree which stands on the body of the Earth, laughs, blossoms and spreads its shade all around. As the sun becomes warmer the cotton plant fibres reveal their silken softness ... so white and bright, slipping into hollow eyes to get absorbed in a corner of the fluttering mind. Silent! Like the tree, however much sunlight is absorbed by the body of a man, the more sensible he becomes. A man who has absorbed much sun is never quickly surprised. To tolerate heat becomes his habit. Fire becomes another name for light. As the road is heated by the sun it becomes more and more empty. The hot, dry winds (loo) of the Indian summer bring desert-like fear with them. The footpath becomes empty of the vendors, as if the vehicle announcing curfew has passed by. There is a silence everywhere. The sun melts the emptiness.

Kishan found that Ramadin, the parched grain vendor, and his almost permanently fixed punctured cycle-trolley had been pushed and hidden somewhere else. In the city the helpless find little or no patronage or shelter. Ramadin stealthily hid his rusted, jammed trolley behind the boundary wall of Kuber Complex and locked it to the strong iron mesh fixed there with his ten-rupee chain and five-rupee padlock, then without any worries went home to sleep at night. He did not run a tea stall, which had to stay open all night to serve tea to those people who came on their way to the station. Even while sleeping he stayed alert all night because he had seen his father's murder. His father's death had woken him up forever. His mother's cries had opened his eyes. His soft hands held no dreams but only the boxes of matches he used to light his chulha (charcoal oven). While he parched the grains he dreamt of burning his father's murderers.

He was short, much shorter than his age. Small, slim Ramadin had one ear much smaller than the other. Ramadin had converted his ear into a hook. He used to hang a key ring with an assortment of keys ... old keys ... strange-shaped keys with the appearance of a bunch of blessed tantric keys. His frayed bush shirt's pocket was filled up like a box. The pockets of his shorts were also full and for this reason rumpled and in comparison with the rest of his shorts very dirty, stained and greasy. The bunch of keys hung safely on his ear. He could not weigh more than two hundred and fifty grams on his scales of chickpeas, peanuts, beaten rice, rice and soaked peas, which he promptly put into the iron roasting bowl (wok or frying pan) filled with extremely hot sand and salt and roasted them. He sieved the grains, poured them into a paper bag, added a small packet of coriander leaves and garlic sauce and handed them over to his customer.

Ramadin lifted up his eyes and asked for a reasonable amount of money according to the goods. He most probably did not charge any customer more than ten rupees. After all, most of his customers who chewed on the parched grains were generally the more needy labour class, who were like lost cattle roaming the street. Along with them were the fourth-class employees found in government offices. At a young age, Ramadin was very mature at his work. His small hands had become experienced much before their time. They had changed through the wear and tear of hard work from being soft to becoming rough and calloused. He talked little, probably as he had experience of a very small world. His whole world was his mother and her small womb-like and safe home.

Kishan took some time out of his job as a salesman in a large store in the newly built Kuber Complex to get a cup of tea. While he was sipping his tea he filled his palm with parched rice and chickpeas from the two-hundred-and-fifty-gram bag he had with him. He passed the time in the shop eating the mixture. One day he asked Ramadin why his coriander-and-garlic chutney tasted better than the parched grain mixture. Ramadin immediately answered, "My mother made it!"

Kishan thought, while passing his time in his new job, "After some time he will say – my wife made it." But then would the chutney be just as tasty?

Kishan remembered the words of the laundryman, who had recently set up on the corner of his street, who, while pressing his clothes one day told him, "Pressing clothes is my business, but no matter how much my business increases my wife will never lend a hand. Today's wives have become madams. Even though my father and my real mother used to wash, dry, press and deliver all the clothes to their customers together." The character of the world today has changed. Kishan had, when all was considered, a simple mother, who had not studied enough to be able to get a job. She was not so shrewd as to be able to fit in with a joint family. Father had not left so much money that she could spend the rest of her life gossiping. All said and done, Kishan depended on her. Kishan thought to himself that if there was anything in this world it was his mother and her home. After the birth of her children, a mother still gives them protection. Mother would always be his armour, even though she was alone and orphaned. She maintained fasts even without water only for the sake of protecting her child. But how much does this starving world give protection? Doesn't time change people in its own way?

Kishan's daily habit was to visit Ramadin's shop, where he used to break his silence and solitude with his questions. He used to pass the time he used to shorten the distance between himself and the answers. He ran the gauntlet of these questions. When Kishan asked where his father was, Ramadin used to answer, "I found out he was dead." He lowered his eyes and head when he answered. At such a young age, answering this probably lightened the burden. How? "I came to know he was murdered." Now he went further. One of his father's customers did it. Why? An argument over the price of the parched rice. In the twinkling of an eye, the argument had become heated and they had started to fight each other, and with his own knife, Ramadin's father had been stabbed in his stomach.

In this way Ramadin was heating his life in his father's parched-grain shop. He could have done other work to stave off hunger, but his earnings were satisfying his life's hunger. Kishan realised his pain that day.

Ramadin's prudence was that his pockets were his safe corner. His keys, which most people used to keep very safely, hung from his ear beneath his military-cut hair. One day Kishan asked him why he kept his keys hanging from his ear just like people hung their keys in the courtyard of their homes in the village; most people in the city kept them hidden away safely. Ramadin answered immediately that they were imitation keys. "The real keys are with my mother. In my pocket there is one that is the key to the girls' box. Brother, this bunch of keys hanging from my ear are my identification, how people will know me in this city." Kishan's eyes lit up with the realisation of this simple truth. The silence of truth stood by this young person and his small parched-grain shop. Standing close to the wall of the Kuber Complex, the air was filled with aroma of various grains like maize and rice being parched along with peanuts and other grains. Kishan remembered the parched-grain shop in his village.

Unlike this one, they were situated inside the house, not unlike the homes of many rich people in the city having shops built into their fronts and also converted into small shopping complexes. It was the smell of the parched grain making the feeling of home and yet it had its floor converted into a place where grain could be easily parched in large iron bowls made only for this and the fireplace built into the ground. All this could make one recognise this as a place to get parched grain, just as the bunch of keys on Ramadin's ear was his identification mark.

In the village the four parched-grain shops could be found in each direction. Each shopkeeper collected grain from the houses in their respective localities. Around three o'clock in the afternoon the ovens were lit. From the homes of poor people or the rich where people used to work as labourers, good people used to gather on the platform situated at the parched-grain vendor's house. The village workers or masters used to gather there, where they used to exchange their problems or their happiness. They discussed their earnings and their losses. Relying on fate with its bittersweet promises, their faces reflected their faults and the sadness of being born in poverty.

In the meantime, amidst the happiness of riches and the helplessness of poverty, there were sometimes loud guffaws and other times soft voices advising people to forget their woes. Kishan was reminded of those times, from the early evening to its end at about seven o'clock. How many stories ... how many truths ... real laughter ... real tears that he used to see and hear there. How the rich houses appeared so upstanding but were in fact only a farce, a lie and unreal. He could see that public platform strewn all over the place. That gathering of all classes was open for all to see, both truth and lies. It was in the labourers' happy kitchen in the parched-grain merchant's house where they could have sattu (flour made from parched chickpeas and barley) made. Sattu and molasses mixed with parched-grain sweets (patti) could be found there. In the evening everything was chewed up there. Nothing had changed in the village or the town. The oven, built in the floor, had changed into the oven on the trolley. Poor men became poorer and were bound by the simple fare.

The fate of children is not determined by their mothers' wombs but by where they are born. The birthplace decides everything; the quality of the soil will decide everything. If it is marble-like ground then so is the demeanour and high quality of the person. If it is painted with cow dung then it denotes a lower category of person. Kishan used to go to work by auto-rickshaw (tuk tuk) where he earned his living. He spent eight rupees coming and eight rupees going home. He changed his auto twice. A young boy used to gather the passengers for the Vikram, a six-seat three-wheeler. Imagine, a child as the driver's helper. Small children doing adult work for their survival, the buttons of their shirts open, exposing the immature chests which their mothers used to caress, now grimy with the daily work, hardened much before their time. Chests to be tickled by their fathers now becoming adult much before their time. Soft silken bodies hardened by the travails of life.

Dirty towels wrapped around their necks and mouths filled with betel, the red juice staining their teeth and even though they had not fully learned how to allow it to liquefy in their mouths still they had begun to liquefy their bodies. Waving their towels, they used to call passengers, like the street vendors selling their wares. Hanging onto the rod next to the seats and with one foot on the step they used to travel at speed along the highway without ever taking a seat, whereas the passengers would hold onto their children whilst sitting inside the Vikram. While calling passengers they spoke with respect: please come, uncle … auntie … grandmother, but then, as if they were the owners, they could be seen berating other vehicle drivers even though the owner of the Vikram was someone else often sitting in luxury somewhere else. They would seat four people in a place for three or keep their luggage on one seat. The passengers always complained to these children but their words fell on deaf ears, and the patience of these children, as their lives passed by, was something to admire. Kishan learnt this art of tolerance and patience from these children and realised how happy they were in their present existence chewing pan and earning money.

One day a middle-aged Muslim man sat in the tempo. He asked the tempo to stop before the regular stop, so the child tapped the roof of the three wheeler and asked the driver to stop. However, the passenger asked them to go a few yards more, near to the butcher's shop. So once more the child tapped the roof, but when the tempo stopped again it had passed the shop, so the passenger gave the child one rupee fewer than the agreed fare. The driver left immediately, leaving the child behind. When the other passengers told him that the boy had been left behind, the driver told them that he would let him walk a while in the heat and learn the value of accepting one rupee fewer. Hearing this, Kishan became angry and asked the driver if he had any compassion. There were such strict rules. Like the military, there was no forgiveness for mistakes.

A person's recognition never comes before they are old, and these were just kids. Kishan watched the boy running like a horse, trying to catch up with them. Inside, he was abusing the driver in his thoughts but was silent on the outside. The stopping place was coming up and the driver slowed down, and the child climbed aboard, laughing without any complaints. He probably knew that if he said more he would hear more abuse or receive punishment. Then a passenger sitting inside said that if that damned old man had got down where he should have and paid the proper fare, the child wouldn't have had to run so far. Hearing this, others started making comments about religion, but this meant nothing to the boy, who thought that he could save the old man having to walk, but brother Vijay took him too far. But still he had to walk. Then at Golgudda, another Muslim man with a child in his arms climbed aboard, even though there was not enough room. It was just a matter of getting in. A female Hindu passenger asked the man to give her his child so that he could sit down. She told him that the child would have difficulty, but he could adjust himself; children are so fragile, she added. Kishan thought that the young boy helper was fragile too. It seemed that poverty did not allow him to be fragile. Along with Kishan, the other passengers looked at the woman and thought that women had no religion or caste – they had only love.

Sunshine ... humidity. At nine o'clock that day the helper boy was not in the Vikram. Not only the vehicle but the whole road was empty. Then the tempo stopped. Kishan leaned forward to see past the driver. The road was empty, but to the left there were three women, their cheap make-up running down their faces. The driver would give them relief; their tiredness would be relived like a good night's rest. They all sat beside the driver without asking where he was going or how much it would cost.

Kishan had arrived at his destination – Ramadin's parched-grain shop. That was where Ramadin, with his key hanging from his ear, lived. That bunch of keys had no padlocks. It seemed as if he had put a lock on his ear and his tongue and hung the keys there. That is why he was silent and probably deaf too.

Kishan took out money to pay the tempo and turned to-wards the compound when Ramadin wished him to arrive. His hand was bandaged, probably because he had an injury. The night before he had been fine. Then the silk cotton tree in the Kuber Complex compound started shedding white balls of cot-ton, just like ice cooling, and being blown by the wind, they fell to the ground. Where would they fall? What would happen? The balls did not know, just as Ramadin did not know, nor Kishan, from the suburbs. Even the child labourers did not know. From the road, the pavement or the drain, if gathered and sold, they would be used to make some rich man a pillow to sleep on. Their flight would be captured. The people mouths would be closed and stitched up, just like the mouth of a cotton-filled pillow. How many lives are sewn up by others, as if they are living clothes just for the use of others?

HABIT

For several days the sound of the wind had not been heard in the room. The bell on the weathervane on the chimney above the fireplace was also silent. A thought that had been playing on Susan's mind, that the sun would come out after a long time, came true that morning. Susan took the day into her lap and became totally involved in it. The day was clear. The breeze was filled with happiness. What more could the residents of a cold country want? Susan decided to enjoy the day's sun. She really liked to walk on her own shadow. Her mind opened up just like her shadow, as if it were her dear Marko's shadow.

Susan wore an overcoat. She wrapped a scarf around her neck to display her beauty more than to protect herself from the cold. She put her gloves on. Her gloves felt like her lover's hand, as he had bought them, along with a cap from Moscow, as a gift for her. When it became cold in the Netherlands she always desired to buy a hat. Marko always told her that he would bring a cap for her from Moscow. Now these gloves and cap brought back warm memories of Marko, which never left her alone. They filled her mind and removed her loneliness. So she found any excuse to wear the gloves and cap so that she could feel Marko's presence.

As always, Susan took Dorp Strat to start her walk. The cars in the park were covered by the sunlight. On the roof of one car, two cats dozed, taking a sunbath. They too had felt the need to enjoy the sunshine like all the others.

As she moved forward a little further, she noticed on the side of the road a woman whom she thought she recognised supported by a rollator and wearing a hat. From under her hat a lock of white hair hung in front of her ear. It matched her wrinkled face and complained of her increasing age. Susan lifted her eyes to the wide glass window in front of which the old lady was standing and saw three cats in various positions enjoying a sun bath.

They appeared more mistresses than the real mistress of that building. There was a dialogue between them, even though their eyes were closed. Susan felt that the old woman with the rollator jealously understood their silence, because the cats were not alone, like her.

Susan turned her gaze to the face of the old woman. She saw that it was Ellie. She lived at the end of her blind lane – she had had a dog which had lived with her for fourteen years. Now it was no longer alive. But Ellie still did not accept that it was dead, no longer in this world. If anyone asked, she replied immediately, "It's got lost somewhere. He'll suddenly come back some day and surprise me."

When the weather cleared up Ellie often went out for walks with her rollator. She spoke to everyone walking their dogs about her dog. He was her favourite. Those who have kept dogs as pets can understand the importance of Ellie's words. She talked about her dog and carried a photo, which she showed to everybody. She gave his description and also handed out her visiting card with her address and asked them to send her dog there, but this year she was more alone, as her two pet cats had gone missing too – these formed Ellie's family of four. She had a photo of herself with the animals. Crying out in tears she said they had left her behind.

Ellie went as far as she could with her rollator. When the weather was fine, she went as far as she thought her dog and cats could have wandered. As Susan progressed, she suddenly remembered a story she had seen in a German newspaper of an old lady who was walking down the road with the help of her walker, being followed by a squirrel which imitated every movement of that old lady as she walked down the street. When she had become tired and stopped and stood with the support of her walker, the squirrel climbed up onto the walker and looked at her entreatingly. The old lady's dimming eyes understood. The old lady picked up the squirrel in her palms. The newspaper reported that they both now lived together.

Susan, thinking about all this, wandered around and finally returned home. After hanging up her overcoat and folding up her gloves and scarf she went into the kitchen. While she was making her coffee, she also spied the man who lived in front of her house. Actually, her house was directly opposite to the man's house, and she could see the front door, garage and garden. She noticed that today the man had brought some newly cut wood on the carrier of his car. This was the same wood that he had spent the whole day trimming from trees the day before.

The winter had begun. The season had caused all the trees to shed their leaves. The frosty cold and icy winds had stripped the trees of their covering, and now the bare branches and twigs were all that remained. That man had first cut down those twigs and then made a bundle of them. He cut them into four pieces using a saw. He then took them to the sawmill at Dorp Strat, where people went to have their wood cut.

From eleven o'clock that man had worn a coat that protected him from ice and water. He had on orange gloves. He unloaded the logs he had brought from Dorp Strat sawmill and stacked them up against the left-hand wall. Then he began to cover the stack, part by part, with plastic sheets, just as mankind hid their desires.

Suddenly she saw two government vehicles busy on the main road that ran next to her house. One of the vehicles had a crane attached to it. As she watched, the crane extended to the high-up branches, just like a giraffe's neck, and brought down several small branches and twigs, then along with the main branches pulled the whole tree down. Slowly, in the same fashion, nineteen trees in Winterkoning were pulled down by the government department. When he saw this, the man thought he had won the lottery. While he was thinking this, in no time people gathered there with their cars and started loading logs of wood into the boots of their cars.

The cold season was beginning to be felt in the icy winds and it appeared that wood would not be available at reasonable prices. Even so, the man who lived in front of Susan's house wondered what had got into the minds of the government. A month before, they had wasted the whole time trimming the trees that had become overgrown on the Langedijk and wasted another week trimming forty-two trees at Winterkoning and thought that they were free of all their responsibilities. But this was not so. Two weeks later, in one sweep, the government department killed nineteen trees and in one park-like plot brought down eight trees with all their branches, but on the other side of the road there were seven trees which were standing, along with the others, and they are still standing there today.

So why? They are of a different type. They are old and frail. Like the other trees they have become sick, and their wood is so soft that it is used for making matchsticks and that is why it is difficult for them to withstand the high winds. Thirdly, these seven trees are sick too. But the government employees, notwithstanding, could not see this, whereas in strong winds not only the branches swayed but the trunks did too. On the other side and throughout the whole of Winterkoning, amongst the other different varieties of special trees, they will always look like refugees. It appeared to the man that now the government employees had become so used to the words "refugees" and "immigrants" that even though they saw the differences they ignored them, because now the whole of the Netherlands had become cosmopolitan in its appearance and behaviour. It is doubtful whether the majority of children of the new generation will have absolutely pure Dutch blood. All the children are of mixed blood, but the cultures will only become mixed once the contradictions are removed. This is why we hear of divorces and separations almost every day. Marriages between lesbian and gay pairs are increasing, mainly because no one really cares about it. All said and done, the man could not understand the logic behind two types of trees on the side of the road, but how could he explain this to the government machinery? Keeping this in mind, he got down to collecting and storing the cut logs and was dreaming of how he could earn some Euros at the same time by selling them, and from his point of view this was not only a gift from the government but a kind of blessing that had been gifted to him.

Susan remembered well that this man had properly inspected his house two months before from the outside. For almost one month the sun used to appear there, whether you saw it or not. The man could be seen moving around his house, sometimes repairing the tiles on his roof, sometimes spending the whole day repairing his wall. Sometimes he would spend his time painting his garage door. In this way, he managed to repair his whole house to his satisfaction. Then he was not to be seen. His car was outside but he was nowhere to be seen. Susan began to think that whilst repairing the back of his house he might have fallen. Had he succumbed to the cold after doing so much work outside? After all, where could he have gone? Because that house was definitely his prized possession: he used to spend all his time working on and cleaning his house, just as a child would spend their time with their toys.

Two weeks later he was seen repairing two bicycles outside of his garage. Susan was under the impression that when finished he would ride off on one and another person on the other, but that did not happen. He sat on one and holding the other cycle he rode off. A short while later he returned, riding his own cycle. The next time he brought his cycle and stood it on the stand at the back of his car. Susan got the idea that he would also put his wife's cycle there too and then both would go off on holiday to Netherlands Besakhenling or Taisil Islands, where they could enjoy the grilled mutton that the restaurants there prepared. The mutton there was famous because it had the salty taste of the air that could be found everywhere on those Islands.

But now what happened? Like a streak of lightening, without putting his cycle on the rack, he sped out of his house, but after an hour he returned with two bicycles hanging from the rack at the rear of his car. He happily took them down, as if he were unloading a load of Euros. On his white face the flush of happiness at receiving a lot of Euros was shining out. In the rush to unload the cycles his hands tightened around the handles, and the cycle bells rang from time to time.

The sun was shining and the wind was blowing. The man did not want to dirty his garage, as it would take time and energy to clean it up and he would earn nothing for his effort. So, as he would get no money for that, he stood the cycles next to the wall and started repairing one of them, and after two hours he put it back on the rack and returned it to the place it had come from.

For the next two weeks the man followed the same routine as if it were a game. Soon Susan worked it out. To the west, on Dorp Strat, there was a cycle shop, and to the east, about one and a half kilometres away, there was another. The village had three schools, several commercial complexes with shops and offices and a supermarket, where people used to come and go on their bicycles. The bicycle was the main means of personal transport for the people here. You needed to pay neither for road tax nor to spend on petrol. In this country there are twenty kilometres of road especially for cyclists. So, people feel that rather than waste money on petrol, the money saved pays for breakfast and lunch for one person. Above all, the bicycle is healthier for people to use.

One day in the evening, the man, after repairing two cycles, stood them up on their stands. Then a white delivery van turned up. The back was open, and it contained sacks of various sizes and weights. These sacks contained potatoes brought from the fields. The driver placed two sacks of twenty-five kilograms each against the wall. The man had made payment. He had earned these for repairing the two cycles. The driver, promising to come the next week, drove off. That potato van came to this house every day. Other vans came to bring cheese, vegetables and other things to a few of the houses. The man's face lit up whenever he saw the sacks of potatoes, as if they were ripe.

The man again checked the repaired cycles and, like a young boy, jumped on one and grabbed the other as if it were a girl and raced off with them, and after twenty minutes he came home. He put his cycle in the garage, closed the garage door and decided he had closed for today. A few days later he could be seen in his kitchen, because that day he would boil his potatoes, otherwise his kitchen, in the dim light of two lamps, always looked empty. There was no life in his oven, or warmth. Nobody came to that house for months. It was not a house but appeared like a forgotten tomb.

That man did not cook anything for himself. His body was just like a skeleton that ate nothing. He bought bread once or twice a week. He would eat from paper towels to save the expense and effort of washing utensils and using water and electricity. He had only three jackets a few selected shirts and trousers. One jacket was for repair work, either cycles or the house; another was for cleaning the car, garden or the rooms.

Susan saw that half an hour had not passed when the light was switched off. The man came out and put his car in the garage. This was the first time he had done that, for from the time he had bought it, the car always stood outside.

Susan went into her kitchen in the morning. She looked out of her window. The morning sun shone brightly. The space in front of the man's house was now occupied by another car. The man's three toolboxes lay open. A red pipe, for washing the car, lay like a snake there. The car had been washed and the man was soaked by the splashes of water being used to wash it.

Susan made herself breakfast and was thinking of making coffee. Last year the man used to leave early in the morning for the North Sea shore about fifty kilometres away, where the town of Den Helder was established, and went to his furniture and interior decoration shop, where he worked all day before returning home. No one knew that he worked there all day. On retiring, he found work to do at home and outside. Susan could understand him repairing cycles and doing cleaning but now he had started to bring cars for cleaning too. He owned a one-and-a-half-million-Euro house. He had his own car. Would he always have to work so hard, even after retirement?

After wiping and polishing the washed car, it shone as if it were his own. Even in the cold, the sweat of hard work always shone on his brow. The sun shone on his happy face. He was happy at the presence of the sun because on this cold day the sun had made his work easier. He was happy that he had found a half-day's work in washing the car. Otherwise, how would he pass his day without work?

INICA

It's falling ... continuously falling ... snow! When the sky is filled with monsoon clouds, there is a different kind of darkness; when the clouds are filled with snow there is a sort of brightness. During such moments, lnica always felt as if the swans were mesmerized in their love play and the white feathers from the couple's own chests were shedding. lnica was engrossed in her thoughts while watching the pair of swans, but today she was duped with surprise when she saw the swans in the river in front of her house raising their necks and watching the sky. lnica felt as if the swans were seeing their own cool feathers falling from the sky and thinking with astonishment, "How can the feathers from my body fall from the sky?' And this sky, how has it become white like our feathers?" lnica saw the changes in nature in her own way and watched them with enthrallment.

Inica was busy working on the computer even during this fascinating weather and her favourite season. In between, she was also looking at the snowfall through the transparent window, which gave a cool feeling to her eyes and happiness of beauty to her mind. When everything in nature and many things of human-made earth are covered with snow and turn white, then it appears as if this is the only truth of life and the world. Along with everything, when the roads are covered with snow, then it becomes difficult ... how to go and from where to go? lnica had come across such moments in her life a number of times.

Before logging off, she checked her inbox. She responded to a few of her e-mails and she also wrote an e-mail to her institute, saying that she would not be able to take Dutch language classes on the coming Tuesday and Wednesday. She also mentioned that she would adjust these classes in one of the weeks next month so that the students did not lag behind. It was not necessary to mention it in the e-mail, but still she wrote the reason for her leave request. Mariam, her daughter, serving at the Dutch Embassy in Harare, Africa, had to collect some historical evidential documents with reference to the Netherlands, and she also required some documental evidence about the condition of women in this place so that she could share the related statement with the diplomats of other nations as well. She had requested two days' leave to help her daughter in this matter, to collect all the readable material and if possible prepare two write- ups and send them to her daughter through e-mail. Really! It is indeed difficult to collect our country's historical–social documents in another country. lnica had explained her situation very humbly in her leave application.

As soon as she logged off, her mobile started ringing. She grabbed it and saw a text message from her daughter. Normally, her daughter would send text messages. She wrote, "Mama, send me your piano. Talk to me in this regard as early as possible." lnica dialled her number, and the voice from the other side said, "Yes, Mama, send me your piano ... I feel very lonely here. Sometimes, I feel desolate in spite of having work. If the piano is with me, I will feel better. I have ordered it from the Foreign Ministry and I have also given your mobile number to them ... they will get in touch with you. Talk to them and hand it over to them. They will pack it nicely and send it to me. This will save you expenditure and you need not bother about the packing too."

lnica was shocked to hear this. Her eyes were sinking with disappointment and dissatisfaction. She was thinking that she was as alone after her daughter left for Harare. Had Mariam, her daughter, ever realised her loneliness? But she did not feel that way after today's phone call. Her daughter was bothering only about her own loneliness. She did not even think that her mother was also alone there. The manner in which Mariam had tried to get rid of her loneliness showed that she was not at all worried about her mother. Asking for mother's piano from her mother, which had the memories of her youth, was somewhat disturbing for her. It had the love tunes that she had sung along with Mariam's father. Even today, lnica played those tunes with her trembling fingers. She played her own tune for her own ears. A long time back, it was her love tune and the same tune remained with her, like the life tune. Even today, she remembered that life tune and thought about the music of her love.

lnica's husband was in love with a lecturer at the economics department in his university. He was the head of the sociology department and wanted to start his family soon. He had proposed divorce to lnica before even knowing about her wishes. He had also told her about his extra-marital affairs.

lnica was stunned to learn about all this. But what was the relevance in forcibly maintaining the relations when there was no love? Her husband was always adamant about his desires and used to impose them on others. She remembered quite well that when he fell in love with lnica, he had hurried the marriage and had not even given her a chance to think about it. When she had to attend an interview in the Dutch language department at Amsterdam University, at that time he had stopped her from taking up the job. He gave the excuse of her being a mother and about her family responsibility and did not allow her to work. He had also questioned the need for her job when he was drawing a good salary. Hence, when he gave the divorce proposal, she had readily accepted it. But she could not come out of that trauma for two years. She never imagined that she would be left alone at the age of fifty-five and that she would have to work for her livelihood and wander here and there in search of a job.

She was killing her time with her piano. The piano was her companion. Her daughter knew about it, but still she demanded her piano. On top of that, she did not think twice before saying that it would not cost her anything or bother her for sending it. Somewhere in her heart, it was pinching. Only the Euros spent were counted as expenditure, but what about the indefinable expenses made on her? She had spent her entire life and dreams in bringing her daughter up. The piano, to which the memories of love moments were attached – wasn't sending it like spending your moments of love? Could there be a bigger expense than what she was about to make?

When her husband divorced her and left the house, the space was empty in her room ... her bedroom ... her life ... even in her body. She had somehow filled that space with her solitude. Afterwards, her daughter had left the house for the sake of her studies and career. She could have stayed if she had wanted to, but no. She also gave priority to her desires and her decisions.

When her daughter left the house, though lnica did not wish it, her space also became empty. She also took away all the things that she needed, even the things that lnica needed. She remained silent. The mother inside her made her quiet. The mother's affection made her calm. Mariam took away the entire cutlery set, the dinner set, utensils and many other such things that had her mother's memories. After her mother's death, lnica used her tea set, coffee set and dinner set very sparingly so that they would remain all through her life. She was living the love of her mother in her childhood memories; she was drinking her mother's love through her childhood experiences. But at the time of going to Harare, Mariam took even these along with her, because they were made in classic design. But what about the empty chair at the dining table, which reminded her about her daughter, who used to occupy it and share the dinner with her? Sometimes, she felt as if Mariam were sitting next to her on the same chair. lnica used to imagine her child sitting on the piano chair. Her tiny fingers, her sweet smile. lnica used to feel her presence even in her absence. But now Mariam was going to deepen her loneliness further and make it even more difficult by asking for her piano. lnica was stunned to hear it. She was scared of the thought of the seclusion that would arise after sending the piano.

It was only the piano that could not go out of the house as per her daughter's wish. It used to start playing merely by her desire. It touched her fingers musically ... it played with her fingers ... it created music and melody simultaneously in her lonely mind. She used to create affection inside herself only with its melody. By creating love from the love that she had created, she used to experience love inside herself. That love which is required to live. The love, whose support makes you experience your own self. The love whose experience gives the feeling of achieving everything in life. It was only the piano that used to play with her. It used to sing tunes with her. With its presence, lnica felt that it would be there with her throughout her life. At the time of her last breath, it would remain silent and sing the song for her farewell from this world. With its presence, she was experiencing her husband's love, touch and smile on one hand and her daughter's flighty at- titude on the other, and a tasteless, tuneless tune, just like that.

lnica practised hard to make it a melodious tune. lnica used to imagine that the same piano would wish her a goodbye at the end as a representative of her husband and family. During times of desperation, she used to wonder if it could appear like a human being, then she would enjoy a heavenly and natural death. But her daughter was ordering her to send it, not even requesting it. Mariam was certainly not aware that she was making her mother so lonely, giving her such a painful stroke by asking her piano from her ... and such a big trauma. She just said "Yes" over the phone.

The officer concerned at the Foreign Ministry contacted her and she called them to her home. They came and took away the piano. lnica was watching her life going out of her body in front of her own eyes. She was silent. Her tears were also silent. Her breaths were also totally silent. Her heartbeats, which used to vibrate at the tune of piano, were stunned. The sorrow of her entire body, the agony of separation from her piano was inside her body. She was fixed like a stone. She did not want to touch the piano, which was going out of her house. She did not want to free her body from the stone form by filling it with the mourning of its farewell. She had usually felt that her happiness had always gone with others, but her tears always remained with her. Her tears had always heard her internal crying and dried inside her.

Even today, lnica remembered her mother and filled her loneliness with her memories, and her grandmother's memories, residing in her. She remembered how her grandmother had separated from her husband, her family, brother and sister in the struggle to protect herself from German invaders during the Second World War. She had spent her nights in sheds which were used to rear the sheep. When the owners of the sheep went out for a while, she would quickly steal something from the kitchen and fill her stomach. At times, she did not even get the time to cook the raw potatoes before eating them. She used to witness the fire from bombshells but could not get even little bit of fire to roast the potatoes.

lnica had always heard the stories of serious struggles from her mother – not the lullabies or the fairytales. During the war, if her mother could get a cloth to wear and a piece of food to eat, that itself was wealth; that itself was money. She never got the chance to see the coins and notes. Her fingers never felt the freshness of notes and numbness of coins, nor did her eyes feel their brightness. Fortunately her mother owned all these things, but in 1953, the rising sea water inundated South Holland and even the sea land province flowed away with it. The sea water flowed several metres above the Netherlands, earth that was two metres below sea level, and lnica became homeless along with her family. Her parents constructed another house in Harlem with her other two brothers. The love and courage of her parents built their home once again. They started a small business with sheep and chickens. They took care of the family. They educated their children. Today, it appeared like some incident, a story. Inside the sensitive mind of lnica lay the history of her mother and grandmother's pain and sorrow, which is contemporary to world history and world wars.

As a mother, lnica remembered the day when her daughter was preparing for the Foreign Ministry examination. She took thirty days' leave for her daughter's studies and preparation; it was leave without pay. She took the financial burden due to her attachment to her child, whereas her husband was a professor in Amsterdam University at that time. He could also have taught his daughter, but he neither had the time nor the patience. He could not spare time out of his seminars, parties and the company of pretty girls. Finally, lnica gave her time for their daughter. She searched for the books necessary for the examination. She ran from pillar to post to find them. She fed important information into the computer. She stored some of it on tapes. She prepared CDs for other information so that her daughter did not face any difficulty and could prepare properly for the examination.

lnica's wishes were also fulfilled along with Mariam's. She got the happiness of success with her daughter's success. After a few months, Mariam was selected and went to Harare. lnica went along with her the first time to arrange Mariam's home. She decorated Mariam's house. She brightened the house with the beauty of a mother's warmth and affection and then came back to the Netherlands, in her deserted and lonely house, to become lonelier.

lnica used to be very sad due to Mariam's absence, as if she has lost something very precious, something that she could not get back even if she wanted to. lnica did not like to stay in that house, but not liking it would not change the situation. One has to change oneself, then the situations change. From that day onwards, she had slowly started to change herself once again. She started getting in touch with her old friends through phone calls and e-mails. She had made it a habit to overcome her loneliness with her daughter's e-mails.

After eight months she suddenly received an e-mail informing her that her daughter was coming to the Netherlands for a fortnight. After reading it, she felt as if happiness were showering from the computer and falling in her lap. She immediately responded, "Stay with me only during this period. I am very happy to know about your sudden visit."

Her daughter replied, "I am coming for an important work-related reason to the Foreign Ministry, so they will make the accommodation arrangements for ten days. For the next five days, Papa has booked a hotel room close to our house in Amsterdam. Still ... on one day, I will take out time for two to three hours in the evening. Accordingly, you should also take out some time."

lnica read the e-mail twice, thrice, but she was not able to believe that what she read was true. She felt as if her breasts had dried up. My daughter does not remember my milk, my warmth, my affection. She does not remember anything ... she does not have any anxiety for me ... to meet me ... no excitement ... no enthusiasm to talk to me. Does she even remember me as her mother?

During her days of unhappiness and nervousness, I used to be awake the whole night. How was her father concerned with his daughter's problems? What did he do when she had a high temperature? Show her to a doctor ... give her some medicine ... everything will be all right. During illness there is pain and restlessness, which the child has to bear, for which the child needs the love of a father and mother. But he had never thought about it. He had never felt the need. After dinner and getting satisfied through mind and body, he used to come home. Had her daughter also forgotten her mother's sacrifices like her father? But keeping aside all her agony, she replied, "I understand your busy schedule. Plan your programme as per your convenience. I will take time out accordingly. But while writing these lines she felt as if she had torn her heart, writing the e-mail not with the ink of the computer but with the ink of her body.

Mariam came to the Netherlands. One day before leaving, she took out time to meet her mother. She met her between three p.m. and five p.m. lnica once again shifted her class timings. She postponed the dates. She adjusted her other programmes accordingly. She was happier to see her daughter rather than meeting her. Meeting for just a couple of hours was not enough ... it was just seeing each other. However, she was getting ready, and it was snowing outside. The phone rang once again. It was Mariam's call.

"I have to see my House Arts (doctor). I have been given today's appointment only and I also have only today's time, because I have to take the flight tomorrow. I have to be there at three p.m. You can also reach me at the House Arts place – we can talk." She could sense order in Mariam's tone. Her phone calls and e-mails did not appear as if she were talking to her mother.

"Yes, I will reach House Arts at three o'clock." lnica controlled her feelings and replied in a balanced tone.

"Mama, please don't take it otherwise ... you are well aware of the situation in Harare. The food and water of that place is like putting one's life in danger. I have always ordered medicines from this place or have been taking them with me. I have to take some antibiotic medicines and I also have slight throat ache. I have vomited twice or thrice yesterday. I hope you understand my problem and will not take it in a different manner." Despite being true, Mariam was trying to explain herself, which lnica did not demand; she did not require her explanation.

lnica was quite upset when she heard all this over the phone. Her motherly warmth had become cool, yet she went out of the house to meet her child. It was snowing ... and snowing. The window pane of her small car was covered with snow. She scrubbed it out and sat in her car. She cleared the front glass with the help of wiper. The road was white, as it was also covered with snow. A thick layer of snow had covered the terraces, grounds, gardens, every place, which was a fascinating view in sunshine and moonlight, but otherwise, the colour white spreads disappointment. When everything used to get covered with snow, lnica used to feel that as long as the snow covered the earth, the earth got some rest. But today she felt that the earth was covered with a white sheet spread on dead bodies. It was snowing heavily. It appeared as if the winds were filling their fists with snow and throwing it on lnica's car and its surroundings. The sheep were also standing, perplexed amidst the snow filled fields, as if they were imagining, "What to eat and how to eat?" lnica moved ahead from the next turn and saw that the water in the rivers, lakes and streams was frozen. The birds of the sky – swans ducks, etcetera – were at the edge of the streets, digging the snow and searching for some food to eat. In such conditions, lnica used normally to carry some food or bread for them so that she could feed the birds wherever she saw them. She used to guess their hunger along with her hunger.

Driving slowly on the snowy, slippery road, lnica reached Amsterdam. She was at the House Arts clinic, where she was supposed to meet her daughter. When Mariam took life in her womb, lnica used to consult the same doctor. It was in this clinic where she learned that she would be a mother. She became a mother when Mariam came into her womb. By becoming a mother, she realised the beautiful, enticing magic of her body, which had become her life's magical fact today and which she could never imagine. When Mariam grew up, in place of her daughter, another new daughter took birth, who used to call her as "mother" but did not know the meaning of "mother". She felt that she was not her own child. Although she had taken birth from lnica's womb, she had got her flesh and blood from her, but that daughter was of her father. She was made from her father's hearty and mental virtues.

First, lnica reached the clinic. Yes, it was she who had reached it before Mariam ... Mariam came into the womb later. Today, the daughter had not come to see her mother; the mother had come to meet her daughter. As soon as she saw Mariam, Inica hugged her. Her heart was beating fast. Her motherly warmth was rolling down from her eyes in the form of tears. Her throat was choked with tears of affection.

The former House Arts of the clinic, who took care of lnica's treatment during her pregnancy, had retired. She had taken care of Mariam not just for nine months but for sixteen years. But now she had been replaced by another new doctor, like a new daughter that had taken birth in Mariam's body in place of Mariam.

Since Mariam had left for Harare eight months back, lnica had been sending her not just medicines but also several other things for daily use. After Mariam's departure, there was news on the television, in the newspaper and in the media about the poor quality of food at Harare, that the people were dying due to lack of drinking water, that life was difficult there. It was almost like hell for people living there; the children's faces looked like skeletons because of malnutrition and lack of potable water. They looked like dead bodies in spite of being alive. Flies crept on their bodies, and their bodies did not have the strength even to make them fly.

As far as law and order was concerned, the situation was so grave that as long as you were alive, you had the feeling of being on the earth. In the past few days, the number of deaths had been rising. lnica's daughter had discovered the reason for this increasing number of deaths. She found that the government was sprinkling some medicine that had affected the crops and the water in ponds, pits, etcetera. This was resulting in continuous casualties which were beyond the control of doctors and hospitals. This news was published with an anonymous name, and it was just mentioned as facts based on research of the Netherlands Embassy. Earlier also, lnica had sent an e-mail to Mariam and had given her original and factual information about this matter. She was very happy to know about her daughter's courageous actions in a foreign country; her heart was full of pride. More than being a mother, now she was proud of her daughter as a mother of a citizen who rose above the motherland and mother's emotional relationship and was working for the protection of human beings and humanity.

There was no e-mail or text message from Mariam for two months. She was surprised yet silent. It might be some kind of diplomatic behaviour on the part of her daughter, she thought. But after a few days, lnica received an e-mail from her divorced husband. "Mariam has expired due to food poisoning in Harare. She had been spending her life underground for the past three months. But it appears that her courageous reporting has taken away her life. Her body will arrive the day after tomorrow. I will send you the flight details. Go to the airport. You will receive all her belongings within one month through the custody of the Foreign Ministry. You can keep them safe."

POWER PLANTATION

"VICTORIA OIL PALM PLANTATION – Suriname Paramaribo" was written in big letters in English on an iron plate. The board was so old that its colour had changed to rusty iron. Somehow, it could be read, with great difficulty. Richard turned his vehicle to the left of the recently constructed new road on the bauxite-red sand road. The same path led to the Victoria Plantation. Due to the morning's rainforest showers, there were potholes at various places that were filled with water. However, he went five kilometres ahead on that same roller-coaster road, which was off the main road. When he reached slightly ahead, he found the Victoria Plantation board once again.

The Victoria Plantation began from this place. Richard signalled from inside his new sports car and once again focused on the path ahead.

There was dense forest. The woods had covered the history of the plantation. In spite of that, the earth was saying something from inside the forest. After moving ahead further, "V.C. 126" was mentioned on an old wooden pole. On moving further ahead, three iron plates mentioning the names of plantations in three directions were found, which were probably very old, and their letters were so blurred due to rust that it was impossible to read them.

Richard stopped his car at that place. Ramaditya and Vedagni stepped out of the car. The sun's heat was at its peak.

Vedagni was busy finding a historical and photogenic location for shooting pictures from her camera when suddenly she felt a terrible pinch on her feet. She looked down and saw a red ant stuck on her toe. She handed over the camera to Ramaditya and jumped towards the car, limping. She sat inside and pressed that toe tightly and started peeping outside. She rolled down the window glass and saw a trail of brown ants on the floor. Her toe was burning severely and she didn't know what to do.

Vedagni got out of the car and saw that Richard was smoking. He was wearing shorts and his company's t-shirt and old rubber slippers on his feet. He was the manager of an iron company that was famous for construction work. His company was involved in making iron frames for the structures for building construction in Caribbean countries. Richard's body and mind had also become like iron in the course of preparing iron frames. But the blue lake of Brinseburkh was also in his mind. He took a dip in it at a few intervals and kept himself fresh. He always worked for the expansion of his company and progress of Caribbean nations, including Suriname, at a global level.

Vedagni offered an insect repellent cream to Richard. He replied, "They all know me very well and now I have also started recognising them properly. I feel that I am also a living creature of this land." There was a smile on his face while speaking the last sentence.

Listening to this, Vedagni remembered that when she went inside a shop to buy this cream, an Indian shopkeeper had asked her, "Don't the mosquitoes of this place recognise you? Because, you are an Indian girl."

After listening to Richard, she questioned herself, "Is it true? Do the insects like mosquitoes and other creatures also recognise the citizens of their land?"

Richard held a second cigarette between his lips. Sweat drops had appeared on his partly bald head due to heat and humidity. But Richard was happy. During the conversation, he quickly took a few puffs and finished his cigarette. As soon as he sat inside the car, the others also occupied their seats. After driving around one kilometre, he signalled and informed them that there was the old refinery. After moving slightly ahead, Richard pointed from inside the car. "This is the main door. Would you like to take some pictures?" He stepped out of the car and stood while asking them. Ramaditya and Vedagni also came out of the car. They went deep inside the refinery till the limit of getting sunk in the forest. They had just taken a few pictures when they heard Richard's voice. "Do not go ahead – there could be snakes, scorpions, anything." They turned back immediately.

Richard had got the car's petrol tank filled at the cell-petrol pump built at the border of Paramaribo city. Richard was very punctual, and he wanted to proceed as per the pace of time, just like the sun.

Talking while driving, they reached Brocopando Lake. On seeing the transparent still blue water, not only Ramaditya's eyes but also his mind became calm like the lake. He went towards the lake along with Vedagni. They both splashed cold water from the lake on their faces, which were damp with sweat. The sun lord was just above their heads. Richard had reached there earlier and switched on the air conditioner of the car so that it would be cool before they came. When they both sat inside the car, they were fresh.

On seeing them silent, Richard started talking about his friend, Mohammed Ali, and said, "He was a very good man. Such people are not found in Suriname, but some enemy from Suriname itself saw an opportunity and shot him first at the back and then four bullets from the side in such a way that he died on the spot. I see that all the good people of the world, whom we think dear, leave us and go. We are left alone. Actually, not only do they die but even we die with them. To some extent, for a few days, they kill us also. But they do not come to know about our death."

At the old bridge situated at Victoria Plantation in Suriname Richard had turned his car towards the left side to see and show the other end of the power plantation. They were passing along a high empty road. During this twenty-kilometre-long inland tour, they came across a couple of huts of forest inmates standing on four high wooden poles. Amongst them, an old probably onehundred-and-fifty-year-old church built in old architectural design was also seen. But even that was dead like the old plantation forest. The church of that area had also lost its identity with the end of the plantation.

After crossing the deserted forest road, Richard parked his car at the roadside. He came out of his car and quickly took a few puffs of his cigarette and asked Ramaditya, "How do you feel after seeing the Victoria Plantation?"

Ramaditya replied, "At this moment, this 'Victoria Plantation' is just a graveyard of the memories of the plantation. The big burial ground of forest. But look, Richard, it is such an irony that our Indian ancestors, who were ploughed to the field along with the plough and along with them even in Mauritius, Trinidad, Guiana, Fiji and other islands, just like our ancestors, the ancestors of Indonesians, of the Chinese, also worked harder than slaves and offered ruthless labour. But these plantations were named as Victoria Plantation, Dutch Plantation, British Plantation ... All over the world, and you will be surprised to know that these people have named even the big lotus of Brazil as Victoria Lotus."

Ramaditya paused for a second while saying this so Richard added, "They are not in power in Suriname at present, but the names of the places are based on the names of the places in Holland, like New Amsterdam is known as Alkar and in some places as Lading Koniginswadus and what-not. This is also like embedding the historical symbols of their power."

Ramaditya agreed with his remarks and said in affirmation, "You are right. In Mauritius, the French colonisers made this rule while leaving power and passed a bill that once we are out of power, the names of these places would never be changed. The same names will continue till this earth ceases to exist."

After taking his seat, Richard took control of the steering of his pick-up Suzuki. He started pulling the wheels of his car once again through the uneven red muddy road. Inside the forest, it was not just hot; it was like fire. There was severe humidity due to the rain at night-time. Continuing their conversation, he said, "Ninety percent of Suriname is forest even today. Only ten percent of the land near the sea and coastal areas has habitation and houses are built, like our land." Vedagni was watching the forests and sharing her thoughts in the same tone. On one hand, there was long, tall grass and bushes and forest and on the other hand, the starvation and poverty of Suriname. She was deeply moved by seeing all this. As she witnessed this, her mind was pinching her deep inside. The earth was producing when it was not getting the seeds for fruits and crops – it was busy growing the grass and bushes. If the people of this place worked hard, then they would reap gold in the form of crops and fruits.

The air conditioning of the car was at its maximum. Richard opened the cool box. He took out three half-litre bottles of Markoosa (a special tropical fruit of Suriname) to drink. He had purchased these from a Chinese supermarket before starting the journey. Almost all the shops and supermarkets of Suriname were occupied by Chinese people. Any uneducated Chinese people took a big hall on rent and filled it with cupboards and stuffed them with goods, and without the knowledge of Dutch, Creole or Sranagtongo language, a money-calculating computer machine was installed and a shop was operated. You may not be aware! When I came to this place, I was affected in a surprising way by seeing the sun's heat at this place, and I talked to some agricultural institutions, which were running a paddy plantation in Nikary state even today.

Palm trees were loaded with fruits and employees were busy harvesting. It was also proposed to a few influential people in government that a solar-energy plant was required in this country: you were reaping gold from within this land itself. So, you would collect the sun's heat in the form of gold. Ramaditya was listening to Richard very carefully. He said, "Actually, solar energy is also a type of scientific modern gold which can be produced for the consumption of the people in the form of electric power. Almost all the houses on Barbados island have solar power equipment installed on the terraces, which produce electricity for the houses. Suriname should take a lesson from this. Two years ago, the Indian Embassy installed traffic control lights in the entire city of Paramaribo which work with solar energy. Besides, it can be used in other directions as well, but nobody thinks about this."

Before Ramaditya could finish, Richard said, "Only when the people of this place are free from eating and sleeping. They are free from work at around two or three in the afternoon and then they go home and eat fresh, hot food and take a nap in the courtyard. They take a bath at sunset and make merry in the city till ten or eleven at night. They drink and spend the night there. Poor people are so busy that they do not even have the time to think about all this." Richard drove his pick-up car through the potholes and jerks, sharing his thoughts. Vedagni felt that Richard was a power plantation within himself, as if he alone were consuming all the solar energy falling on Suriname's land.

The vehicle turned towards the Bransberg road. After going slightly ahead on the same route, there was a path leading to the goldmines. Mining used to take place as per government norms and was given on contract by the Suriname government to Canada.

New roads had been constructed and were ready to use in these areas just recently. This contract was given to China. Driving his car at the speed of one hundred and thirty kilometres per hour, Richard said enthusiastically, "Thank you, Chinamen … whatever it may be, you have at least given good roads to this wild country in the name of development."

After four or five kilometres, the same bumpy road was found and Richard stopped his car. He came out and lit his cigarette. Smoke through nose and plans through mouth, this is Suriname.

Richard got back into the car as soon as the cigarette was finished. He started the car and said, "It's an eighteen-kilometre-long uphill drive. Seven kilometres is fairly easy, but after that it is difficult, and there is no road on that route. The road is so narrow that vehicles can pass through from both the sides with great difficulty." He had just finished saying this when he saw a few vehicles coming back on that route. Richard reversed his car half a kilometre. There were valleys on both sides, hence, stopping your car close to the edge of the road was like inviting trouble. Still, Richard had no option and stopped his car almost at the edge of the road. Along with a few cars, a minibus also passed through, which had children aboard, and they were all very scared and sitting quietly, just as Vedagni was, sitting behind. Suddenly, petrified Vedagni noticed a weaver monkey. It was holding a basket. This monkey was named "weaver" due to its basket-weaving art.

Richard stopped his car as soon as he saw it. The basket-weaving monkey came and sat in front of the glass fearlessly, and due to its actions, it was passing its hand towards Richard and Ramaditya from the other side of the glass. Richard pulled down the front-door window on his side and stretched his hands outside, offering the bread pieces that he had brought for their meals. The monkey took his share immediately and moved ahead.

Richard started the car. The monkey turned back and saw.

Ramaditya waved his hand and took his leave.

Finally, the car reached the Bransberg hill. All three of them were tired due to the bumpy uphill drive, in spite of being in the car. Richard had a tough time driving the car and one could see the fatigue on his face. His face was red and the drops of sweat on his face were appearing as if he had just washed his face with water.

As soon as the car reached the high mountain area, a Surinami leaped towards their car and stood. He asked them to pay for visiting the place and parking and offered them a receipt in return. He had plaited his curly long hair and tied it up on his head; it was no less than a small black mountain on his face. Everything was resting on his fat blunt nose. He gave a receipt for seventy-five SRO Surinamian dollars. Richard parked his car. All three of them were standing in front of the famous calm blue lake.

On seeing the lake, Vedagni started thinking – Bransberg! Once upon a time, this was the golden valley of Suriname. Today, it is famous as the Blue Lake. It gives a soothing effect to the eyes. These people crossed the red path and thick forests of Bauxite to the north of Jilandia and reached this place. The dense forests that covered Suriname have somehow protected the bauxite mines. Nature is a watchman for protecting nature; otherwise, human beings would have crushed her a long time back, nature and her monstrous form. The foundation of Suriname's land is laid with bauxite and gold mines.

Richard told them that the mineralogist, Browns, was the first person to have discovered this hill-top of Suriname. He explored the golden valley sand mines. He got the roads constructed – therefore this place was known by his name. The rain and water sources in Bransberg, other than its golden valleys, was not just water but it also had the herbal effect of other plantations along with the effect of gold plate, hence, it was not just water but a stream of gold.

Ramaditya held Vedagni's wrist and all three moved towards the lone restaurant in that area. They occupied the chairs placed along the table kept in the corner. They were experiencing the cold on the hilltop of the lake. They ordered Parbo-beer, which is the production beer of Suriname.

The so-called Surinami waiter banged the one-litre beer bottle on the table and went back. He also placed three large glasses on the table. Richard poured the beer into the glasses. The froth came to the top, just like the anger that rises in the mind on hearing truth and lies. Richard once again started the conversation and said, "I would like to say something about myself. I was born in the Netherlands. We are three brothers. But we all are different. Our father was very ruthless towards us; therefore, all three of us have achieved something in our lives today, and hence we all remember our father with great respect in our own ways." He finished his words and picked up the beer glass and took a sip.

"What was his name?" Ramaditya asked Richard with a lot of respect.

"Father Simon. Today, I call his name. I can speak from my mouth, but during my childhood, I used to only hear with my ears. There was no question of calling his name from my mouth and uttering it." While answering, he touched his ears and shut his mouth with his hand. He continued, "If my father asked us to enter our room once, then we would enter his room only when he called us. We were so petrified about the fact that he was our father that we could not think about anything except what he liked. I was ten years old. I used to get five guilders for washing and cleaning my mom's car and eight and a half guilders for washing my dad's car. His car was three times bigger than my mom's car and I had to clean it from the inside as well. I worked continuously for one year in this way, but, one day suddenly I gathered courage and asked my father, 'Mom gives me five guilders for washing her car, but why do you pay just eight and a half guilders for washing and cleaning your car? I clean it even from inside.'

"He heard this and just said this much in response, 'It is my decision.'

"'Then fine; I am not going to wash it from today.' I turned and came back. When I did not wait for my dad's answer, he went out to get the car washed. After two weeks, I realised that my income had reduced. So, I once again went to my father, gathering courage. I spoke to him and beseeched him, 'I will start washing your car again.' I had forgotten about the self-respect of childhood and asked.

"'Fine, but you will get just five guilders now.' My father was taking full advantage of my helplessness. It included the unique learning of today's tough world. I spent my childhood with a father of that kind. But even today, I remember him with immense happiness. I feel proud of him and admire his strictness." The wet sparkling of those memories could be seen in his eyes.

The big bottle of beer had been finished with this talk. Nobody realised. They ordered a second bottle. Once the beer was served in the glasses, Ramaditya remembered his father and said, "My father was an Indian farmer. He was born in Suriname. He obtained the teaching of religion and education from his ancestors who came from India. He had strong faith in religion. I obtained the knowledge of Ramcharitmanas and Gita from my father. He made me read Ramcharitmanas and Mahabharat along with him. I sowed paddy, tied bundles; I was the flock man for the cattle. He used to keep a part of his income in a corner inside the cupboard and used to tell me that I was the eldest son of the family and to take money from this place whenever required, but I was not to touch this money for wasting it. Just imagine that money is not kept here. You will embrace sin if you use the money lying here for some wrongdoing.'" Ramaditya narrated his father and his childhood briefly.

"But how did you settle in Suriname?" Vedagni wanted to know in spite of knowing about it a little. Meanwhile the so-called lunch was also served. Three pieces of chicken, salad, khuswanti (Boda) and rice in a bowl was served. Everything was served on one plate and put in a heap. In spite of being freshly made hot food, it had no fragrance. But all of them were hungry, and it was three o'clock in the afternoon. They somehow swallowed the food along with talking. Vedagni left more than half of her meal. She was willing to starve rather than eat that food.

She once again filled her glass with the beer froth. All of them turned towards the lake to get immersed in the beauty of the nature. Richard pulled out a cigarette from his case, lit it and started talking.

"When an advertisement for the post of manager of this company was released, I responded to it and came to Suriname from the Netherlands for an interview. Nothing could be guessed from the interview, whether I was selected or not, but the owner of this company, who was two metres tall and would be certainly more than one metre wide, took me towards a canal of Sarmaka along with his three friends. There were fifteen to twenty Katiya (the name used by Surinamian Indians for the equipment used to catch fish) in everybody's hands. They were catching fish, one after another, very swiftly. I had just one Katiya given by the owner, but till five in the evening I could not catch even one fish. On top of that, I was baked under the sun and was almost half-dead. Then he ordered everybody to pack up and leave. In the meantime, a big fish was caught in my Katiya, luckily. A smile spread on my red baked face. At that moment, the owner of the company put his hand on my shoulder and said, 'I select you for the company.' In this way, the owner of that company kept me under the hot sun of this burning land of Suriname for the whole day and made me undergo an acid test to get selected. I'll never forget that." While saying this, Richard took out another cigarette from the wooden case.

"And what about this marriage – love? When and how did all this happen?" Ramaditya wanted to know, because the previous night he had treated his family to dinner at Khazan, a restaurant. His three children, Pooja, Lakshmi and two-year-old Tarun, were present along with his wife, Shyama, who had also brought her older unmarried sister, probably to take care of the children. Everybody was supposed to take their meals as per their wish in buffet style. Drinks and ice-cream could be ordered, which were separate from the fifty-two Euros charged per person. Both the women took three helpings and ate a stomach full. The first time, they had filled their plates with fish salad. The second time, they took fried fish and vegetables. After that, ice-cream and drinks were separate. They did not just fill their stomachs with food; they had even filled their minds. They were fully satisfied with their meals.

Vedagni was surprised hearing all this. She would not have been able to eat with people who ate food in this manner. Instead, she would have remained hungry. For her, food meant fragrance and beauty along with hunger and taste. She felt that in India, for people eating in this manner it was said, "They had mind-satisfying meals."

PROFANE

There are several religions in the world and those religions also have many religions. However, nowadays only one religion is heard and seen, and the funniest part is that the heads of this religion are not heard anywhere. Usually, the people of other religions, media agencies, newspapers and magazines and books raise their voices and talk against it. The name of this religion is Islam and its people are Muslims.

Due to its actions of terrorism and violence it is under the constant vigilance of the government, and the terrorists in turn are watching the people in government. Power and government are the goals of terrorists. The so-called revolutionists and think-tanks talk against the Burkha system in order to come out of the conservative approach of Islam. On one side there is the backwardness and narrow-mindedness of religion, and on the other side there are dark clouds of war surrounding the sky with the fear of terrorism and extremism. This was a matter of concern for Gayatri. She had been busy reading Gita, the Quran, the Bible and other religious books for the past several months. She wanted to read the book titled "Quran", written by Vinobaji, the great leader and founder of the Bhudan movement. Finally, she was able to find that book from her personal library.

Gayatri always wondered why the Muslims and terrorists didn't ever feel that the Hindus and Christians had always protected the followers of their religion. A Hindu and Christian never behave with a Muslim in a manner that is inhuman and which shows some differentiation, as if they are doing some injustice or atrocity, but even then, why are Muslims so cruel and unkind towards entire mankind? When Vinobaji's book on the Quran was being published, at that time he was on his tour in Pakistan in with respect of his land movement. When the news of printing this book in Kashi was made public, the newspapers in Karachi made a great hullabaloo. There were many reactions against it at other places too. Actually, science has reduced the size of this world, because it wants to bring everybody closer to each other. If mankind remains aloof and every society considers itself superior from the other and looks down upon others, who will tolerate it? We need to understand others properly and accept one another's qualities. The first sentence in the summary of Vinobaji's Quran reads, "What is the spiritual knowledge of Islam? I have selected each point of it and kept it in front of all the religions and tomorrow it will be in front of the world."

Gayatri was lost in these thoughts when Akhilesh reminded her that it was time for her ambassador's farewell party – did she want to attend it or not? Gayatri started thinking. What could she say? She was well aware of the farewell parties of ambassadors, what they were and how they took place. She was silent and she maintained that silence for some time. Akhilesh said, "Come on, let's go. When a retiring officer is met on the last day and given a farewell then he or she feels satisfied."

Gayatri gave her affirmation with a "Yes", and Akhilesh said, "We will not go emptyhanded. We will pick up a bottle of champagne at the store." Gayatri was still silent and Akhilesh once again added, "Okay, so let's buy a nice bouquet of flowers from a florist on our way." He suggested this as an alternative.

"What will he do with a bouquet? He will be gifted so many of them that there won't be any room to keep them. Then he will send it to his junior's place. What will he get? What will we take along?" Gayatri rejected this idea on the basis of her several years of experience.

"Okay, so gift him a book." Akhilesh proposed this idea as per her choice. Gayatri liked to give and take books as gifts. But she was silent and continued to think. She recalled everything. Officers working in foreign embassies usually donated the books gifted to them to the embassy library. These books were kept lying in a corner, because in foreign countries neither the books nor the newspapers were sold for scrap.

The books were dumped in a corner like nameless things, awaiting eyes to read them and a place to be kept, and in due course the books were destroyed by termites and moisture. Gayatri remembered one of her previous postings. She had requested the opening of a room in the basement. She had noticed that the books were kept there and were lying like dead bodies. A few were kept in cardboard boxes and a few in big jute bags, published by the publication department of the Ministry of External Affairs, the Department of Hindi and the Indian Cultural Council. These books were sent for free distribution in foreign countries for propagating Indian culture, literature and Hindi language. But these books were lying in that place. Termites had eaten those books to such an extent that it was ordered to burn the books in order to save the almirahs and the room. As per the order, all the books were gathered and burned. After coming back home on that day, Gayatri cried a lot, as if she had seen the burning pyres of live humans, something that was prevalent during the Sati system in West Bengal. That day Gayatri tolerated the pain of books just as Raja Ram Mohan Roy would have tolerated pain during the Sati system. Therefore she did not agreeing to gifting a book. She kept quiet. Akhilesh was also mum.

Gayatri looked at her watch. She placed a bookmark on the page containing the synopsis of Vinobaji's Quran and went to get ready. Akhilesh was already dressed for the event. He said, "Get ready fast; we should keep a two-hour margin."

Sometimes, when the clouds changed their shape in the sky, rice-grain-sized snowflakes started falling. Akhilesh and Gayatri parked the car at a place amidst the snowfall and went inside a reputed bookstore. They had to select a book for an ambassador who was being given a farewell. He was retiring from office due to his age; otherwise he was perfectly fit and healthy. Gayatri wanted to pick the gift very carefully, with the aim that the book should be taken along with the ambassador. It should not face the negligence of the embassy.

First, she glanced at the books in the fiction section and then rolled her eyes over poem collections and saw that the poems had been written on men's handkerchiefs, vests, t-shirts and also on cups and plates. Prior to this, she had seen paintings made out of cups, scarves, t-shirts, pens and the like in Van Gogh and Rembrandt museums. But she was impressed with the poems written on handkerchiefs, t-shirts and serviettes. She had seen the poems of a Dutch poet on the serviettes of the Iskheltama restaurant. She remembered the Surinamian poet, Dabru. The prints of his poems and face marked on t-shirts were sold, and the sales girls and boys of the bookstore showed their backs with pride and placed the poet's collection in the customers' hands.

"Do you like any book?" Akhilesh came close to Gayatri and asked. "Have you selected any?"

Gayatri responded, "No. I feel that your selection would be better." Akhilesh gave her the right to select.

Gayatri was wondering whether or not a religious book would be better. There are several thinktanks all over the world talking about religion. They have created a good market for themselves in the world of books. A few of them pose as the masters of the modern brain. With these thoughts in mind, she was standing in front of the religious books section.

The books related to Islam and Christianity and occupied several racks. She found the Sanskrit and English dictionaries in the Hindu religion. The remaining books were related to Buddhism and philosophy. In the past ten years of her experience, she had realised that books on Buddhism were replacing books on Hinduism in the world. Since the day that the incidents of struggle between Hindu and Islam religions have come to light, both have created havoc. This has not harmed the Muslims as much as the Hindus globally. Terrorism took birth from Islam, but the global Hindu was known as violent. The Hindus at the centre of power in India are probably unable to understand that due to their so-called perceptions, the existence of Hindus and the pride of Hinduism are endangered at a global level. Buddhism has taken the place of Hinduism. For example, while staying in a room in Berlin, the capital city of Germany, Gayatri pulled out a drawer and she saw books on the Old Testament, the Bible and Buddhism. She prayed to those books, considering them as the God's feet.

But she was thinking that during her Japan tour last year, she had experienced with a lot of reverence that the Japanese had projected most respectfully not only Buddha but also the strength of Hinduism behind it. Japan has given the highest respect to the Hinduism of India, Indonesia and Thailand at a global level. The Sharain of Kyoto city, the Vedas and Upanishads have also been mentioned as a collection of the verses of philosophy of Buddhism written in English and Japanese languages. Even in this age, the Japanese still possess simple and knowledgeable honesty. However, leaving aside the books on the Hindu world and Hinduism, Gayatri picked up a set of books written by American philosopher Stephen Knapp – *The Secret Teachings of the Vedas, Facing Death: Welcoming the Afterlife, How the Universe was Created, The Universal Path to Enlightenment* – and shared her decision with Akhilesh. But he was a holding a book titled *The Clash of Civilizations and the Remaking of World Order,* written by Henry Kissinger. He had bought it for himself.

Gayatri had attended several farewell parties of ambassadors prior to this. She was aware that i t was nothing but an untrue celebration of dedication and efficiency. Officers would praise the ambassador just for the sake of it because they were forced to do it. The officers, who were literally vexed with obeying the orders of the ambassador attended the farewell parties half-heartedly, as they were aware that once the current ambassador left and the new ambassador took charge, they would get time to breathe a sigh of relief, and in between, around six to eight months would pass.

On the other side, the ambassadors never got tired of cursing their junior staff and trying to find ways to get out of there. They were fed up with their inefficient staff and did not know how to find a way out. In many instances, they felt that it was better to write a letter and send an e-mail in place of dictating a letter and checking it several times.

Really, the high officials of Indian government were simply remarkable. The governments of around twenty-eight states in India were unable to handle the Pandora's box of languages and religions. On top of that, the scenario of foreign embassies was such that one officer was a Brahman and the other was from a backward class; a third was from Tamil Nadu and the fourth was from Orissa. The mixture of languages and religions, the ego of regionalism, all these things did not allow the development of team spirit in the embassy. Everybody was fighting with one another inside the office. They shook hands with others and smiled due to the attachment for the dollar, the Euro and the pound. These smiles were so artificial that even the real teeth of people appeared uglier than artificial teeth. Howsoever healthy and attractive Indian officers would be, whether the officer was a male or a female, due to their hypocrisy and two-faced behaviour they looked ugly in front of the Europeans, Americans and even South Americans. They were neither able to make eye contact with others due to their hypocrisy and duplicity nor others wish to make eye contact with them. The eyes do not connect as such where there is falsehood, deception and fraud. The eyes have a strength that can easily recognise truth without any effort.

Wassenaar was the city of residence of the affluent people and officers in the Netherlands. The farewell party arrangements were being made in a small castle of Wassenaar. Three institutions associated with the embassy were supposed to take care of this event. From the chairpersons of the business institute, cultural institute and creative institute to the secretaries, all were coordinating with the embassy secretaries and other officials for this purpose. As it was the so-called "intellectual farewell party", the wives of the officers of the institutes were not present, plus a dinner was also planned for this event. Otherwise, the people brought along not only their family members but even their guests. The preparations were going on till the last moment and till such time that the ambassador arrived at the venue. The senior officers were moving their eyes all around and inspecting the arrangements to ensure that everything was perfect. Junior officers had no work but were simply hanging around pretending to be busy. It was all nothing but a drama. The ambassador, who was supposed to arrive at seven o'clock, arrived suddenly at half past seven. All the preparations came to an end in a surprising way as soon as he arrived. The embassy officers took their positions such that they would definitely be noticed by the senior officers and the ambassador. He entered the meeting hall with an artistic smile and wearing a mask of humility over his proud face. His personal assistant ran to the coordinator and asked him to start the programme immediately.

The sequence of speeches began one after another. The heads of the institutes were singing the ambassador's praise. People were feeling short of words to complete their speeches. The ambassador was feeling proud of himself, listening to the people. His heart was giggling with pride. The ambassador had arranged foreign tours for Indian-origin officers to the institutes made in other countries at the expense of the Indian government. Sometimes he used to invite them for dinner parties during the visits of higher officials of the foreign ministry or Indian ministers to his country. He had been luring the officers of foreign institutes in this manner and then made them do and say whatever he wanted. The offices of Indian embassies and high commissions were these days the pastime spots for ministers and higher officials of foreign ministry. On one side, they were always on the look-out to go to a foreign country at the expense of the government. On the other side, the officers of the embassy waited for an opportunity to flatter the ministers and superiors to get a better posting. It was an irony that nobody from the home country was able to notice all these things.

Thanks to video applications and PowerPoint programmes, the task of flattery has become easy nowadays. Everybody wants to be seen on the screen and now every department appoints a photographer. A woman walked with the senior officials like their vanity bag. The secretary of the ambassador arranged all these things in a very dramatic way and it appeared as if the minister, secretary and ambassador did not like such a kind of cheap publicity. They did not like photography at all, but the camera flashes kept on going, photographs were shot, smiles turned into laughter and the people continued to watch the show and clap their hands. The unappealing show of diplomacy took place in front of everybody, but nobody commented about all this.

After the so-called marvellous speeches of the heads of three institutes, the laptop button was pressed and the process of a slide show with smiling faces began. The photographs of the visits with ministers and leaders were also shown. On seeing these pictures, Akhilesh recalled that when he was posted in Panama, Sarveshwar was also posted there after a year. Two months after his arrival, a minister visited that place. The officers from Washington D.C. to Panama were on their toes. The accommodation arrangements were made at a five-star hotel; a dinner at the ambassador's residence along with a dinner with affluent people of the city was arranged.

The officers of the embassy and Indian foreign ministry were busy round the clock with this event, along with phone calls, e-mails and faxes. Everybody was running on toes whether it was a weekday or weekend. Statements were being published in the newspapers every day and tall stories were claimed about improving diplomatic relationships between the two countries, but when the minister arrived and his personal assistant proposed a female night companion, the secretary of the ambassador started shivering. He could not do it without permission. How would he ask the ambassador? But the new secretary was unaware that the ambassador was also a shrewd man. He had arranged a lot of things for others and a lot of things for himself.

As soon as Sushil, ambassador's secretary, came close to him and bent down to say something, the ambassador guessed it and said, "I understand. All right, arrange for it, no issues. Just ensure that the man is fully satisfied and remembers his visit forever." Sushil felt that probably this was the first time that the ambassador was speaking to him so affectionately. He did not know much about the minister, but he wanted to obey his ambassador and get into his good books. However, he was not aware that he would have to sacrifice his wife if the ambassador showed an interest in her in order to protect his job and Panama posting. If he refused then the ambassador would use any allegation and send him to India, along with his family, like a parcel. At that time, the government and the officers did not bother about the expenses of the Indian government or about the feelings of the secretary if he was forced to return to his department within six months. But everything was meaningless in front of the ego of the officers.

Akhil remembered that his friend had told him once about two instructors for yoga and kathak dance working in the Indian cultural centre affiliated with the Georgetown Guyana Embassy and both were unmarried. Being unmarried proved to be an advantage for practising these arts in the initial days. The yoga instructor, Sadhna, had been working there for one year and the ambassador admired her physical fitness. Sadhna had also agreed to his friendship. Sometimes in the pretext of walks and at times in the name of parties, the ambassador started spending his time at her residence in the morning and evening. Nobody dared to speak about it in the embassy, but everybody knew about it. However, they kept quiet.

After a few days, the kathak dance instructor, Kavita, was appointed in the Indian cultural centre. The beauty of a dancer is normally flawless. The beauty of the face and the attraction of the body are fascinating. Moreover, the expressions and physical movements of a kathak dancer are extremely beautiful. Kavita was an elegant woman with a gifted beauty and dancing style. The ambassador's eyes were always keen to catch a glimpse of her. He used to call her to his room with some excuse or other. She used to talk little and quickly leave in the name of practice. The ambassador's wife, Kanchan, also started admiring her. Kanchan used to find ways to invite Kavita to her home. Kavita wanted a female friend in a foreign place so that she could at least get rid of her loneliness even if she did not get affection. She liked Kanchan's friendliness. She started enjoying their friendship. The ambassador used to spend his evenings with Sadhna, and Kavita used to spend her time with his wife. Both were overcoming their loneliness.

The friendship became very strong within two months. One day, Kanchan opened up in front of Kavita and told her about the relationship between her husband and Sadhna. She also revealed that she was very upset about it because the whole embassy, the whole city knew about it and people used to talk normally about it at parties. Kavita was very angry on hearing this and she revealed to Kanchan that the ambassador called her to his room and looked at her with a different intention and also that she did not allow him to come close. Kanchan was shocked to hear this. She was surprised. She was the wife of a respected and prestigious Indian ambassador, whose behaviour was like that of a low-level ordinary man. How would the embassy staff and officers respect him? What would his driver be thinking about him? How could he show respect towards him? If he did not respect the ambassador then why would he respect her? Everybody was tight-lipped just to save their jobs. She became extremely sad and unhappy and stopped attending parties with her husband.

One day, the ambassador had an opportunity and lost his temper. Kanchan could not stop herself. She told him directly about his behaviour with Sadhna and Kavita. The ambassador was furious after listening to everything. Kavita had never fallen into his trap and now he had to hear this allegation. He could not tolerate it. He made some staff members of the Indian cultural centre make grounds for her character assassination and sent her back to India. He did this in order to lead a normal family life and also carry on with his colourful life. Kavita was innocent and a close friend of Kanchan. She did not keep quiet after going back to India. She filed a case of defamation. She appealed to the Women's Commission and also wrote to the Ministry of External Affairs. Her only mission was to tell the world about the misdeeds of the ambassador and get back her self-respect. The evening time that she used to utilise for her stage shows and theatres was now being used in meeting lawyers and high officials. She stopped wearing her anklets. She would be able to wear them only when she was free from the clutches of defamation. She would be able to express the love of Radha and Krishna through her forehead only after removing the lines of tension from there. She had to clear the dark spot on her character and then decorate it with a red spot, a "bindi". These feelings had changed her direction altogether.

There was loud applause. Gayatri returned to the hall in the castle in Wassenaar, where the farewell party was going on. Before inviting the ambassador to deliver a speech, his personal secretary did not want to lose this opportunity and started singing his praise. He said that the ambassador has set an example in establishing cordial relations between people and that he had maintained an atmosphere of family freedom at the office too. Gayatri was shocked to hear this. It was so difficult to even get his appointment. It was very difficult for the Indian-origin people to meet the embassy's people or any of its officers. Voluntary non-government organisations liked to invite them as chief guests. But they did not get a quick response; they gave some excuse about the arrival of a minister or some high official, hence the whole Embassy was busy and they did not even have breathing space.

Besides honouring and taking care of Indian high officials, leaders and ministers, they developed a closeness with the leaders and queen of that country in the name of getting fame and showing some programmes. Otherwise, in the remaining time, the Embassy people were busy arranging facilities for themselves and taking care of themselves in the foreign countries. Most of their time was spent in their children's admission and their education and settling medical bills and city travelling allowances. Their time was lost in finding ways to earn extra income, the old habit of Indians, because they are always bothered about converting Euros into rupees and calculating their net income. So much so that they even hesitated to buy a cup of tea, because two Euros was nearly equal to one hundred and forty-five rupees. Their pockets were full of Euros, but their minds and hearts were occupied with rupees.

Well, after hearing words of praise for himself, the ambassador stood up and once again started talking about himself in a very diplomatic way and talked about co-operation. People's ears and eyebrows were raised. They were trying to establish direct eye contact with the ambassador through all means and hoping to hear their names in the ambassador's speech. The junior officers and staff members of the embassy were probably not aware that the ambassador was not a God, though he was all in all in the embassy. The Almighty was someone else.

The applause could be heard at intervals. The so-called punctual ambassador was himself late by an hour. People were continuously talking about his love and affection. But Gayatri was also aware of some truth. Once, she had visited the embassy in normal clothes and she saw an office boy sitting close to the guest room window with a mobile stuck to his ear. He was sitting there so that he could inform the embassy people about the arrival of the ambassador, so that they could be alert and he too could take his position and salute the ambassador.

As soon as the ambassador's car entered the office premises, he jumped like an animal in the circus and warned the staff on the ground floor and informed the staff on other floors through the phone. Afterwards he stood at the door like a statue and opened the door, took the bag and file from the driver and moved towards the ambassador's room. The ambassador shook his head and started inspecting the reception area in a very dramatic way. Nobody was there except Akhilesh and Gayatri. The book rack was also empty, although the Hindi department and the cultural department of the Foreign Ministry sent books worth millions of rupees every month to the embassy, besides countless magazines, newspapers and other reading material. But these were not displayed in the reception area, as everything was available on the internet.

The guests and staff members were habituated to taking dinner at seven in the evening and were waiting till nine o'clock in the small castle of Wassenaar city and showing signs of restlessness. The officers of the embassy were taking a bite and sipping some drinks quickly without getting noticed. They were drinking tea and giggling before the ambassador's arrival. But as soon as the ambassador walked in, there was absolute silence.

The programme was going on. After the ambassador's speech, people thought that the programme would come to an end. But, at that time only, the personal assistant of the ambassador distributed pamphlets in the front row, which were passed on to the other rows as well. It was the first page of a book. The release of a book was announced. Once again the mic was in the hands of the ambassador. He was the editor of that book. He narrated the story about the struggle for publishing that book. He praised the institutions for their support and the cost of publishing and the efforts of the Foreign Ministry. Like a computer programme, the pages from the book and the ambassador's photo on the pages, pictures with the prominent and important people of the Netherlands were part of the body of the book. The book was titled *The Saga of Four Hundred Years of Struggle of the Netherlands and India*. The book was published within a period of six months with the articles of writers and researchers of the Netherlands' universities and institutes. The co-author of the book was also present at this occasion.

Normally, the publication of a book took around six months, but this book had been written and published within six months in a very surprising manner. The writer's guild of this vicinity was sitting in front of the wall screen. The pages of the book were being shown on the screen through a projector, and the author of the book was describing the book in his own words. He had probably forgotten that this it was a foreign land and not India and that the guests were not employees of his embassy who would sit there for hours without bothering about food. At the end of the programme, it appeared as if it was not a book release programme but a book exhibition event. The

ambassador was displaying a broad smile of personal achieve-
ment and satisfaction on his face and took a special seat in the
first row. Gayatri wanted to gift him the set of religious books,
which she had bought with so much effort, and leave. By the time
they could reach him, people were already standing in a queue
to meet him. Gayatri also stood up. Her husband also followed
her. They were both against all these formalities, and many a
times a person lives such movements forcibly and gets fed up
and ultimately it shows on their face in the form of disappointment and desolation.

The two people standing ahead of them had also gifted books.
The ambassador took them in his hands and simply passed them
to his secretary; he did not even look at the books. Moreover,
that gift was given to him by a Dutch couple. He should have
shown at least this much of courtesy at the time of his farewell.
But when Gayatri saw that the ambassador was not honouring
the gifts of foreign guests, then why would he respect her gift?
Moreover, the immigrant Indians did not get any respect in the
Indian embassies of foreign countries. They had to run from pillar to post to get even ordinary documents signed, just like the
Indian officers who were accustomed to forcing people to visit
their offices a number of times for simple work. They behaved
in the same way with the Indians living abroad. But they could
not share their problems with the officers in foreign lands, because they were the officers whom the Indian government had
appointed to listen to their grievances and resolve them. In the
Netherlands, anybody could get an appointment with officers
in government offices and hospitals through a single phone
call, and the officer concerned would receive the guest at the
reception on the given date and time and take the guest to his
or her office. Tea or coffee was offered, and the work was completed as early as possible. There was no question of commissions or donations.

Akhil kept his hand on Gayatri's right shoulder and signalled
her to move ahead. But Gayatri saw that the ambassador's secretary put the gifted books on the floor, and she was upset about

it. She quickly pushed the book into the bag hanging on her shoulder; she did not think about the time that she had spent buying it. Gayatri picked up a copy of the ambassador's book, which had been released a few minutes ago and moved it in front of the ambassador for his autograph. The ambassador signed it with a proud smile on his face and said, "Please get the embassy stamp on it."

"'Stamp' means 'seal', but why?" Gayatri moved to a corner and whispered in Akhil's ear.

"Because it has the ambassador's signature. How can his signature be verified without the embassy's stamp? The person who reads the book should know that the ambassador's signature looks like this," Akhil replied in a light tone.

"So, he wants to leave the last signature of his office with the embassy stamp," Gayatri said in affirmation but added, "The same signature is present in his editorial also, where his designation is mentioned. So why is a stamp required?"

"Some things do not have any logic," Akhil responded to calm her down. "Let us take a quick round and leave – it is already eleven o'clock. Snacks cannot be a replacement for dinner. We have to go home and prepare some food." Akhil said it very light-heartedly to change her mood.

"Kindly put a stamp below the ambassador's signature." Gayatri opened the page of the book in front of the officer for the embassy stamp.

BIRTH

Hanika woke up as usual, although it was not necessary, as it was Saturday. She could have overslept if she wished. But as was her daily routine, she was habituated to waking up at this time, so her eyes were wide open. How long would she keep lying on the bed, changing sides and forming wrinkles on the bed sheets? In such situations, wrinkles would form more on the sheet of her brain than her bed.

She got up from the bed and went into the kitchen. She boiled water in the kettle. She kept the so-called tea bag, it was called "Juthoute", containing mulethi, or liquorice herb, in the cup, poured hot water in the cup and the tea was ready. Making tea is so simple. Ground powder of any flower, leaf, herb or seed is being sold as tea. The business of giant companies and sips from small teacups. Had everything been like today's tea then life would have been so easy!

She sat in front of the computer with her tea and switched it on. She used to check e-mails from her old friend every morning. This was an old friendship, but in spite of being old there was no depth in the friendship to be so called "old". But looking at the time she called her an old friend and exchanged e-mails once in a while. Sharing news about her two children, she wrote, "My cabbages are growing well and they have started going to school. You are aware that I am their only guardian in the form of a single parent. Bringing them up amongst my project work is certainly challenging and at times I feel tired with my life. Even then I don't have any complaints with my life. In a way, I have the pride of being self-made." She continued about the expansion of her project, and she had added a few interesting attachments.

Normally, Hanika would start thinking seriously after receiving Sofia's e-mails. They both called their children "cabbages" in the normal Netherlands parlance. But Sofia's two cabbages were from two different countries. Sofia had gone to South Africa for a project. She would feel lonely after working for the whole day, so she used to take an early light dinner and go for long walks. After walking for about two kilometres, she would stop at a fruit shop. She used to drink fresh orange, pineapple and sometimes grape juice. She used to buy some fruit for the next morning. he owner of the shop was an old man. Still, he ran the shop somehow throughout the day just to maintain the tradition of his father and grandfather. His son used to handle it in the evening after coming back from his job. After studying philosophy, he did not get a respectable job and started and instead started working in a mill, which required more of his labour than his intelligence. His philosophical mind was always looking forward to talking to someone, and Sofia's mind, tired of loneliness, was always anxious for conversation.

As the night extended, the number of customers reduced. They used to talk to each other for several hours. Usually, when her eyes started blinking and she could not speak due to yawning, she would start walking towards her flat. Her project was about to finish when suddenly one day she realised that she had fallen in love with the son. The next evening, she also realised that she had turned forty now. Who knew when she would find a person with this kind of friendship and deep mutual understanding! With this expectation in mind, she started developing a strong friendship with Aliphira and within a month, along with their hearts, their bodies also came close to each other.

After two months, Sofia had to leave Durban. She wanted to give shape to her work as well as her friendship and in the meantime she discovered she was pregnant. She was very happy from within. She wanted to witness the magic of her adult body. She began to experience internal changes taking place inside herself: a satisfying lethargy, a mind that was eager to taste different types of food. There was pleasure and relaxation and a lot of other things besides, but she did not have time for these things, as she had to complete her project.

When Sofia completed her work she came back to the Netherlands, her hometown. She met Hanika and told her about her pregnancy. Sofia informed her parents that the father of her child was Surinami. Her parents were also happy to discover that their daughter would become a mother after a few months. Sofia named her child Neko. His face resembled his father's, but his eyes and complexion resembled his mother's. His hair was also like his father's, dense, curly hair, which stuck to the scalp. Sofia was a botany expert, and she usually said, "Hey, the hair of a Surinami Surinami looks just like the forests appear from an aeroplane – button-like and sticky. Well, it must save the expense of haircuts. A lot of shampoo will also be saved, as there is no need to wash his hair daily." She used to say this and laugh out loud. She became a mother at the age of forty and that too from a negro. Sofia did not have any photographs of her child's father.

When she had been with him, she had not felt it necessary to take his picture. When her son was two years old, Sofia told him about his father and his country. Neko memorised it as Africa … Africa. One day Sofia showed him a Surinami Surinami man and told him that his father looked like him. From that day onwards, whenever Neko saw a negro, he used to start shouting, "Af-rica … Africa." He had a springy walk like his father and sat in a squat position.

Sofia wrote to Hanika by e-mail, "Children probably learn more from their genetic code than their external environment. Neko's father is not here; he has never seen him, but I see his habits in Neko and I am puzzled."

Sofia got another project. She had to visit Germany frequently. She used to take Neko along with her. She used to breastfeed him. When it was time to feed him, she never bothered about her surroundings. If someone was present in front of her or not, she did not hesitate to feed her baby. She had to visit a lot of countries, but she did not get a chance to visit Africa again. After a few days, Hanika received an e-mail. Sofia wrote that Neko was four years old that day and that she was pregnant for the second time. "My pregnancy is two months gone. I am very happy to know that I will be a mother again. I had told you before that when Neko was born I dreamt that he would have a brother. And look – my dream has come true. The father of this child is Dutch, but he works in a factory in Brussels. Hence, there is no chance for him to live with us. But he has neither any regret nor disappointment for this; even I do not have a problem with it. I will take care of both the children. I am happy and thank God that even at this age I have produced two children. I will at least not be lonely or keep a pet to kill my loneliness. My parents, and especially my grandmother, are very happy. She tells me that whenever I have extra work during the weekends, leave the children with them. They will take care of them. Thank God that he has blessed me with two beautiful children."

Sofia used to call her two children cabbages from two countries. While reading this e-mail, Hanika remembered that last year when she went to play golf, she had played a nine-hole game three to four times with a lesbian couple and she had found out that the two girls were living together. But one of these had physical relations with her male friend and gave birth to twins. Now, these two mothers were bringing up those two boys. The so-called father visited them once in one and a half years. But the children were not aware that he was their biological father. They only knew their two mothers, and these two mothers knew that man as a sperm donor, in just the same manner as one buys something when it is needed, as if someone buys a seed to sow in the soil.

Hanika felt that such women bought seeds to cultivate the soil of their wombs. This was the fruit of their bodies and would be known by their names.

It was a holiday. But the city centre was open that day. Hanika went out on holiday. She sat alone on the terrace, facing the sun, and took two glasses of beer, roamed here and there and came back home. She took a deep, refreshing hot-water bath in the tub and prepared dinner while listening to music. She enjoyed coffee after dinner and got back to her work. At that time, her telephone calls were also recorded on the answering machine. Usually, she did not answer the phone in the evening or night. She did not want any kind of disturbance or conversation while she was working. She loved her work and she did not want any hindrance in that love.

Before leaving the house the next morning, she listened to all the recorded phone messages. After getting ready and taking breakfast, she then responded to the phone calls. She took the keys to her cycle and went out cycling on the roads. Sunlight ... splendid sunlight ... the forthcoming season has started spreading its bright light. The spring season had started filling the Earth with the warmth of its beauty along with the sunlight of the month of April.

On every side of the roads and in the green-grass fields at the highway crossings, yellow tulips had sowed the plants of spring over the entire land of the Netherlands.,. Many varieties of yellow tulips may be found, and Hanika had seen a few out of these in Belgium and Luxembourg. In addition, one could see the yellow fuchsia bushes, rising to a height of one to three metres, spreading the brightness of the spring season. These were bushes without a single leaf, just vivid yellow spring flowers, very flowery and the bushes so dense that one could not even see through them.

When Hanika watches these fuchsia bushes, she wondered if anybody had so much fun ... beauty ... intense happiness in their lives. On seeing the flowers, she felt that the same amount of beauty, happiness and pleasure could be experienced through the eyes in a moment while watching the beauty of fuchsia flowers, and this pleasure was also enough for that particular moment. The bushes of fuchsia flowers made her forget everything. She went cycling five to seven kilometres just to see these flowers, and along with that she also saw the fields of sheep, because during this season, the ewes gave birth to lambs, which appeared as if white and black flowers were falling from their mothers' bodies. For some time, those white flowers which had fallen from the bodies of the ewes converted the green grass field into a field of stars and the lambs looked like sparkling stars. Hanika always loved watching the love between the newborn lambs and kids. She enjoyed watching the little lambs insisting on their mothers' milk, the mothers then after giving their milk pushing them off to graze in the fields. In this process, they used to stop for a while and watch Hanika.

She liked to meet these sheep and lambs instead of chatting, writing e-mails, talking over the phone, visiting someone or inviting others, because the affection that she got from them was not available in any relationship or conversation. There was an odour of selfishness everywhere, just like the odour that is felt at the time of cutting grass or cooking, which cannot be avoided.

It was four in the afternoon and the city centre shops would be open till nine at night. This happened once a week in all the cities of Holland and similarly on the first Sunday of every month. Hanika loved to roam in the cities, roaming alone, roaming unrestricted and watching the crowd. She experienced a sort of affection even amidst unfamiliar and unknown people; she felt that her happiness was also included in their smiles, in their laughter.

The spring season is officially announced in the Netherlands from the 21st March. Hanika wondered why the queen of this country felt that the arrival of seasons on this earth was also dependent on her whims and fancies, whereas once the ice started melting, from the month of February, the sun lord stretched his arms of rays and took in the earth and pampered it in such a way that the earth started flourishing and blooming in the warmth of its love. The tulips appeared on the roads, footpaths and crossings in the form of a notice of the arrival of the spring. The lambs, resembling the white flowers, were also delivered from the bodies of the ewes in the green grassy fields during the same season. Even then the country, the radio, the television had to see spring with the eyes of the date declared by the queen. She inaugurated the world-famous spring garden of Keukenhof on the 21st March for sixty days and gave it to the flower lovers for safe conduct.

However, Hanika was at the city centre. The sunlight was bright and shining. As per the media and also the weather equipment hanging in her drawing room, pleasant weather was predicted, and as per the prediction the colour of the weather would be yellow and golden, as if the sun had coloured the earth with its yellow colour and the earth had also filled the sun with its yellowish beauty.

It was not noon yet, but the middle-aged people had filled the open terraces of small and big restaurants. They were sitting with their faces towards the sun like the sunflowers. They were wearing sunglasses to protect their eyes from the ultraviolet rays. They put their jackets and mufflers on their chairs, while some kept them on their laps, slightly between their thighs. Most of them had unbuttoned their shirts to reveal their chests, especially the women, and they were taking a sunbath to tan the skin of their chests and hands.

Hanika liked this. Like others she also opened her hands, thighs and chest to darken their skin tone and included herself in the crowd. The dreams and happiness of the crowd were very intoxicating for her. Shre got involved in the happiness of all and buried the time of her loneliness in this way. She did not feel lonely; she always wanted to be with herself because she believed that if a person stayed with himself or herself in the true sense then she or he would never feel lonely. We have eyes, dreams, ears and all the sense organs. We have realisations, desires, heart and mind; then why and how can we be lonely?

She again remembered that it was the 21st March today and the first day of spring. The clouds had also allowed the sunlight to come in. The sun was also welcoming the spring. Both had an affectionate smile for each other. Hanika accepted this invitation of nature. She kept her bag on a corner chair on the terrace. She hung her overcoat on the chair and kept the muffler neatly. She opened the first two buttons of her shirt and stretched the collar. She exposed part of her neck and chest towards the sun. She moved her fingers in her hair from front to back twice – the hair was combed. She usually used to comb her hair in the same way. She ordered a coffee and also a few pastries. She finished her coffee after some time. She continued to sit there.

She kept watching the human bodies in a way that she could still understand their inside. In one of the auto cars of the city centre, special European musical instruments were being played; the whole street echoed with them. Hanika moved towards the tune. She came across a flower shop in the middle of the street, which was set up only in the morning. A card was tied on a ribbon wrapping a bunch of roses, tulips and other flowers. Hanika covered her neck with the muffler and when she was passing through the flower shop, an old woman smiled and gave her a flower with wishes for the spring season. Hanika saw a card with that red rose flower, which was announcing the birth of a new flower shop on the first day of spring, as if that shop had also taken birth and blossomed like a flower in this spring season on the roadside, next to the footpath. For Hanika, this was similar to the people who sent cards to friends, relatives and colleagues when they changed residence. They sent cards to their close ones when a baby was born. Hanika took the flower from the lady and thanked her, and she started searching for the smell and smile of spring in it with her blue eyes, as if the blue sky were bending over the flowers.

As usual she went inside a clothes store. She visited DD, Zara, Mango, SPS and other international brand stores. As soon as she stepped inside the store, she saw an old, well-dressed, healthy woman sitting on a wheelchair watching a young model. She put her eyes into the young model's eyes, making different postures, sometimes touching it. She was engrossed in various kinds of discussion with it. Hanika saw all this and stopped. Mooi Model – "Beautiful Woman". "How lively it appeared, as if she were sitting here to talk to me only." When Hanika heard it, she felt the enticing attachment of the old woman towards the model: "She talked to me", but that too was about the model; she was so mesmerised by it. Hanika said "Tatsinse" (See you again) and left.

She went around from one shop to another, enjoying the crowd, dissolving some faces in her memories, playing and coming out of some scenes. The church bells reminded her of the time. It was five in the evening. The shops were open till late evening as it was a Thursday, and today they would be open until nine. The restaurants and pubs were open till midnight every day. It appeared as if the people had learned to be awake the whole night from here only.

The wind was blowing heavily. The clouds were also seen. The atmosphere was becoming cool. Hanika decided to return home. While returning she passed through the same shop where the old woman was talking to the model. Hanika noticed that the old woman was still talking to the model and even now had a feeling of contentment while doing so. Hanika stopped there once again. She stood outside the shop and noticed that unique scene. The woman noticed her. "I come here daily after taking lunch at my old house and talk with this model girl for three to four hours. She is a model: she cannot walk; she cannot go outside the shop. She is sitting here only for me. She is in more bondage than me; she is more helpless than me. I understand her difficulty; therefore, I come to see her in my wheelchair. I see her clothes being changed every week. She is dressed in the same clothes for the whole week. I want that she should wear different types of new fashion clothes every day. She should be happy. She should have no complaints. Look, the shop is stuffed with new clothes. I am myself helpless. I need the help of nurses to take a bath and put on clothes at the old house. When I was a child, I used to change the dresses of my dolls every day and take them for a ride on my cycle. Now I cannot even move without a wheelchair and this model is imprisoned in this shop. I feel pity, on myself and on her. What can we do? I remember my childhood, dressing my dolls every day. When I tell the salesgirl of this shop she says, 'She is a model, not a living girl, and we do not have so much time.' This salesgirl does not understand anything. She has no emotions."

Hanika expressed empathy towards her and then moved towards the parking area. She inserted a coin in the parking meter. The cost of parking for four hours was twelve Euros, which was more than eight hundred rupees in Indian currency. She deposited the parking money and took out the card from the machine and sat inside her car. She started the car and drove out of the parking lot. Her attention drifted towards the radio – a news bulletin was being broadcast at that time. The news read that a woman had delivered a baby at the parking entrance on her way to hospital. The girl gave birth when her father pressed the garage button while driving and took the card. The vehicle was parked immediately. The nurses came from the hospital, a stretcher was brought, doctors came and rushed her into the hospital and the umbilical cord was separated.

The birth of the girl and the time was the same as that of the parking ticket, which contained the date and time. The news reader said that they had talked to the mother. They were both healthy and he said that his colleague had reached the office late, as his car was stuck in a traffic jam. It was rush hour, as everyone was rushing towards their homes after work. Hanika was shocked on hearing this news. With this incidence of birth, she remembered the birth of Sophia's children and how and in what conditions children are born. How they are brought up with great difficulty, the women taking care of them, because they have delivered these children. They are the mothers of these children. The children are part of their bodies, the live form of their blood and flesh, finding a way to live in a forest of human beings. But she felt, why only the children? She was also finding the path every day to live in the forest. She faced the challenge to protect herself from the dangerous animals in the form of human beings. Only she was aware of it and her soul. Somebody else gave birth, but the difficulty of living throughout the life had to be borne by that person himself or herself. She thought in her mind, "Is this called birth?"

SAVITRI

Savitri was unable to understand certain things, although she could have easily denied this. There was no need to compromise and tolerate such things. Yet, things carried on in this way. For the sake of this acceptance, people accept certain things and convince their minds through logic, especially with respect to relationships. She felt stunned watching the people around her. She could not sleep the whole night and continued to wonder whether she would have been able to tolerate these things if they happened to her.

Anand's Chinese friend had come to receive them at Amsterdam airport, because when Anand contacted his son from Suriname, he confirmed the same and said, "Santa Claus will be arriving in his village on the same day. I will have to take the children and go there, but, no issues, Stella will take them. I will be at the airport."

When Savitri found out, she said, "There are so many people in your company. Moreover, you have so many friends; anybody would be glad to come and receive us. Why are you troubling the poor boy? Santa Claus is a very enjoyable movement for children and they get such an occasion only once a year." Savitri gave her views compassionately.

As per her wish, Anand was trying to speak to one of his friends in this regard, and she recollected that last year when they had visited the Netherlands, Santa Claus was present in the vicinity of King Alexander and Queen Maxima. Both of them were present there with their three daughters. They were carrying their children on their shoulders and standing amidst the crowd. As soon as Santa came close to them, they moved slightly forward to shake hands with Santa Claus. They shook hands with him and moved their children's hands slightly forward to shake hands with him. The king was carrying his two young daughters one on each shoulder. The sisters sat facing each other. Sitting on their father's shoulders, the girls were happy to see the hats and heads of the people, and the king was happy carrying them on his shoulders amidst the crowd. Queen Maxima made her youngest daughter sit on her shoulders and hang her feet around her neck. Queen Maxima was holding her feet firmly. Her daughter was four years old at the time and had just begun her schooling. She was clapping her hands and expressing her happiness.

Savitri was also very happy to see all this. She remembered her own childhood. When she was a child, she also sat on the shoulders of her grandparents and visited the village exhibition called "Mela". Many times during pilgrimage tours, she used to sit on her grandmother's shoulders and tried to make way with her sweet voice and little hands. She used to reach the threshold of the temple through her grandmother's feet.

Looking at the enjoyment of King Alexander and Queen Maxima, Savitri recalled that like every year, last year also, there was an exhibition of artists and book sellers at Bergen in North Holland. Be it a shop of fancy clothes or a saloon, a magazine shop or a gift shop, huge paintings made by the artists of North Holland were hanging in all the shops. Extraordinary pieces of art decorated the roadside, the circular street of the church, restaurants, bookstores, etcetera. Artists had hung their paintings and removed everything after sunset and left the place. At the same time, book-sellers and book lovers, having large collections of books at their homes, were also selling their books. This was similar to the sales activities that took place on the birthday of the queen of the Netherlands. People brought unused things worth collection: children's toys, clothes, shoes, and put up shops along the sides of the roadsides of the central church of the city for one full day. They reached the place the previous evening and booked their places, and the family members decorated the shops into the wee hours. The government provided all kinds of facilities for them for this purpose. Higher officials of the city centre also visited the market and shook hands with everybody while greeting them.

Attractive white-coloured tents were put up on the ground all around the fashion stores in the centre of Bergen. Tables were placed in queues below them and piles of books were kept on those tables. It appeared as if those books had received an invitation from the art exhibitors. Savitri was looking for a collection of love poems from the piles of those books, whereas other various subjects were stocked there. However, one of the book vendors told her, "There is a collection of love poems written by King Alexander and Queen Maxima." He put a book in her hands written in the Dutch language. The title of the book was *"J" "A", meaning "Or" meaning "S" meaning "Yes"*. Savitri liked the title a lot. Only the word "Yes" is so wonderful to share between two lovers for love. "Yes" is only "Love".

Savitri was sitting on a chair. She was lost in her thoughts when Anand told her, "Ita has instantly agreed to pick us up." She proceeded to her house with her Chinese friend.

It appeared as if the fire were showering from the sun on the land of Suriname. It was covered with heat, and the land of the Netherlands was covered with snow, as if the feathers of white swans were showering and the chill were seeping from their feathers. It was so cold outside the car that it felt as if this cold were not only outside but also getting inside the body one layer after another. The body was also becoming cold along with the earth and there was a feeling of shivering inside Savitri's body. Anand was talking about business, his friends and family to his friend in Dutch. He came to know about his so-called second wife, because they were not married, but they had two children. She had not returned from Shanghai for three months. Savitri had suspected their relationship since last year. Both used to visit China but separately. When her husband went to China, she used to stay back in the Netherlands and when she went to China, her husband stayed in the Netherlands. A short Chinese woman and an old lady used to come to Savitri's house to sweep and mop. The Chinese woman had three grown-up children, who were studying at university. She used to say that people did not normally marry in their community. Men kept several women. Most of the relationships did not last for more than three to four years and one man became the father of children with many women. Similarly, one woman gave birth to children by several men. The situation was similar in the Chinese community living in Suriname, and also in the Surinami community of Suriname it was very common. Nobody had any negative feelings towards either the woman or man in the society.

With this thought in mind, Savitri started looking outside from inside her car. It was snowing more heavily. The ground had turned white with snow, as if the earth had covered itself with a white blanket. Herds of sheep were standing baffled on the ground, carrying the burden of the snow in their minds. They usually dug into the ground and grazed on the fields or slept on the ground while grazing. But today they were feeling deceived due to this continuous snowfall, because the grass was covered in snow. How and what could they eat now? Savitri was watching everything from inside her car and could guess their concern. However, it was not enough to understand their pain and problems. It does not end with it; one could only express sympathy towards that concern.

Savitri reached home. She was trying to remove the gloom which had spread inside the house, which had been left alone for almost three weeks. The flowers in the flowerpot in the drawing room had dried without water. It was a cloudy day and Savitri could not determine when the sun had actually set. It was four o'clock in the afternoon, but darkness had spread completely. Everything was surrounded with it. She could hear the chirping of birds from inside her house. As they did every year, a huge flock of Siberian birds had migrated towards the south and warmer regions to protect themselves from the cold. The noise of the flying birds would resound in her ears for several nights. The dread of the flying birds, due to the fear of cold, would cause Savitri to shudder deep inside. With this sight, she also remembered the butterflies, which hatched in Canada and which had to fly up to the forests of Mexico once their wings had grown in order to save their lives. They continuously flew for up to eight weeks to reach their destination, just to protect their lives, for the sake of protecting their species.

The next day, before dusk, Savitri and Anand reached the De Flakhels building. De Flakhels means "birds" or "lots of birds".

Conversation – relationship – touch – love – taste and happiness.

These are the words of life's hunger and pain, providing completeness of life.

After entering the De Flakhels building and climbing up the stairs, Savitri used to climb up and down the stairs of these words also and reached her mother-in-law with Anand. It was almost a year since she had been climbing up and down the ladder of these words. Savitri came out of the lift. She was looking through the length of the corridor when she noticed that the doors of room number 515 were partially open. Her mother-in-law was standing with her body partially inside the open door. The eighty-five-year-old had blurred vision but her brain was able to understand the entire world very clearly. At times she used to remove everything and keep aside and sometimes she maintained silence. But her gestures communicated everything.

She could sense the arrival of somebody and thought that probably it could be Savitri and Anand. She strained her eyes as she looked into the corridor and as soon as she recognised them, she commented, "You haven't been here for a month ..." There was sweetness in her complaint.

"Oh, Mama, we were here to see you just three weeks ago, before going to Suriname," Anand replied to his mother while kissing her on her forehead.

"How's it going on there?" Her tone was somewhat firm.

"Don't ask me anything, Mama. When I was there, my heart was shocked. The heart breaks. Suriname has changed a lot now. It is changing every moment. People have become very dishonest. People promise but do not complete the work. They take money, but do not deliver goods on time. The goods that they provide are cheaper and of poor quality compared to the prices they charge. The floor that we had constructed developed cracks within a month. I was deeply hurt after seeing all this. What has happened to your country? Just tell me. The people's morals are degrading day by day, be it at home or outside." Anand went and sat on the single sofa which was lying in front of his mother while sharing his views. He always preferred to sit on that sofa.

Savitri touched her mother-in-law's feet and looking into her eyes, she said, "Mother, look into my eyes. I have brought the water from Maikhanta Canal, which flows in front of your house. There are fish too, if you can see. You can catch them if you wish." Savitri could not say that they contained the love of her son and herself because she wouldn't have understood the meaning. When there was no response from her side, Savitri added, "Please, smell me!" She brought her forehead close to her mother-in-law and said, "You will feel the fragrance of the soil of your Suriname, in which you cultivated paddy for about fifty to sixty years and that country became your own country. Listen to us; you will hear the heartbeats of Suriname, the voice of birds and the tune and melody of songs." Savitri finished her point in the flow of emotions and giving support to her mother-in-law's shoulders made her sit on the sofa. Mother had not yet sat properly. But she could not stop herself from speaking. "You have not brought any vegetables along with you like gourd, bitter gourd, beans and crackers. You did not bring fish too?" The taste and temptation for these things could be clearly noticed in her voice.

"No, Mama, nowadays the security checks are done very strictly. Even at the time of check-in at Jandrai Airport, they open each and everything and check, and whatever appears to be suspicious is simply thrown into the garbage bin without questioning. At Schiphol Airport in Amsterdam, the security dogs start sniffing as soon as you disembark from the aeroplane. We have heard that special arrangements are being made at Suriname Airport also. Sniffer dogs will be used for the purpose of checking. This is happening because of drugs. When the cauliflowers and cabbages are small, drugs are inserted into them by some technique and when they grow big, people carry them to different places. From the time two men were caught doing this, all types of vegetables, fruits and fish are cut and checked at Amsterdam Airport. I am ashamed when I see all this happening in front of my eyes. This is a great insult. Therefore, your son believes whatever is to be tasted should be done in Suriname itself, for how long can we bring and store it in Holland?" Savitri had explained everything in detail to make her understand. But mother's opinion did not change.

So she spoke as soon as Savitri finished speaking. "Your Pran, Manu, Manoj, Leena, in fact everybody brings suitcases filled with these whenever they come. They bring fish sufficient for one month and all the families of these Indians living in The Hague and Amsterdam fill their bags and inform of the date of meeting by telegram to all these people and these people go and buy everything from them. They store it in the deep freezer and it remains in good condition for several days, even months." Mother was expressing herself and the temptation for these things could be felt in her voice.

Anand responded immediately, "One should not eat the old, stale food." Anand wanted to give his view forcefully.

The pain and anxiousness of waiting helped mother remain young even at this age. Though for a few minutes at least she opened the door, waiting for her children, whereas the old Dutch couples were normally found lying on their beds and watching television. They were aware that nobody from their family was going to visit them. They did not have time for all this. The new generation did not need them and probably the old generation did not require the new generation. Therefore, the old people of the old house had created and established a new world of relationships for conversation. They experienced the love in it. They held each other's hands, sometimes kept hands on each other's shoulders and at times touched cheeks and lived their happiness with the touch of closeness.

Anand's mother went to the bathroom. In the meantime, Savitri thought of pouring a glass of orange juice and heating the rice and dal in the microwave that she had bought for mother and also boiled water in the electric kettle to make tea for herself and Anand. Savitri had just begun to do all these things when she heard a scream coming from the bathroom.

"Bacchi ... hey, Bacchi, please listen!" The voice was quite sharp. Savitri was extremely scared to hear it and thought that mother might have slipped.

"Just look at this – my panties have become wet. Give me another pair;, they are kept on the top shelf. The sisters keep them there." Her mother-in-law had requested it very humbly. Savitri understood that her panties had become wet, as she had waited some time. Mother pressed the flush button. Savitri moved forward to change her panties.

"Listen, my child – please give me a bath. The sisters just pour water; they do not scrub my body. It is itching a lot." Savitri's mother-in-law had opened both her mind and body in front of her. Savitri made her sit on a plastic chair and gave her a shower with hot water. Mother's mind was wet along with her body. The pain on her face, which was tired due to waiting, was relieved. Savitri could imagine that mother was becoming wet with both water and love. She was feeling satisfied. Savitri took some Dooze gel in her palms to scrub mother's body properly. She scrubbed mother's back, chest, thighs and legs gently and was about to clean her feet when mother said, "Put some gel in my palms. Let me clean my body thoroughly." Mother had requested this very politely. Savitri understood that mother wanted to clean herself thoroughly and the term she used for it was "body". Savitri kept the soap and gel in her palms and was wondering that mother used such decent words and even today, in spite of living in a Dutch community, she used the word "Lahanga" for long skirt and "Odhani" for scarf. She removed her scarf only at the time of taking a bath. She wore it even when she went to bed.

One day Savitri was kidding with mother and while making her lie down on the bed, she said, "With the fear of leaving home in your dreams, you wear your scarf at night also."

"No, no, my head never remains uncovered." Mother had presented the document of her dressing.

She was living in a Dutch society and old Dutch people were living in the rooms next to her, and she used to interact with them too, yet she did not develop any affection for that society. What was considered as backwardness in other's views were the values of ancestors for her and she felt very proud of it.

She had taken a bath and Savitri had taken a bath with mother's happiness. She wiped her body thoroughly with a towel. Savitri had just turned to the other side to pick up her mother's gown when she said, "Hey, look – my ribs are giving me a lot of pain. Please rub in the ointment." Mother requested once again.

Savitri stretched a little to reach the ointment on the rack and started to apply it to her dry body. "We can only apply it with our hands; we cannot rub it nicely." Mother was expressing her limitations due to old age and inability. Savitri massaged her ribs as she had asked and was about to hand her gown to her when she made another request. "Please scratch my back; it is itching." She turned her back towards Savitri and stood. Savitri started to scratch her mother's back around her shoulders.

"Slightly to the other side ... a little above ... a little to the right ..." mother went on and Savitri kept on moving her hands as she was instructed.

"Ah! Yes. Here, my knees a giving me a lot of pain. I've applied ointment several times during the day – what can I do? Please apply this pain-relieving balm on my knees. I am unable to bear the pain." Mother pleaded once more. She was thinking about the pain in her lower limbs and wanted to get rid of it. Savitri felt that her legs had borne the pain of eighty-five years. It appeared as if the entire history of the pain of her journey of life was passing before her eyes once more. The bones of these legs contained the intolerable pain of risk standing against all odds.

Mother was unable to separate herself from her past even though she was living in the Netherlands. Since she had grown up, she remembered all the events from that day till today as if they had happened only yesterday. Mother used to tell Savitri, "Look at my fortune. When I was just sixteen my mother handed me over to someone else. She only brought me up and performed my marriage. When I went to my in-laws I had a step moth-er-in-law. I did not get a mother there either. I have grown up without a real mother.

"When I became capable of working then I had to cut the crops and work in the fields until two o'clock at night. We used to put a wooden plank on the floor to sleep at night; all of us at home too. I used to go home just to take a bath and finish other chores and then used to be in the fields once again." She used to say, "I used to wear clothes to knee length and sowed paddy in the fields. They was easy to work in and comfortable. My body used to get wet with sweat because of the entire day's work. As soon as it was dark mosquitoes and other insects used to bite and my body became red. Don't ask me anything; you don't know anything. You have neither sowed paddy nor any other crop. The sorrow of growing paddy in a foreign land. The fields were our own but we had to slog – labourers were not available. At that time, the queen ruled in that place. She used to dictate. On top of that, I used to give birth to children every second or third year. Take care of my young son – feed him. I used to put the children to sleep at a height and go back to work under the scorching heat. One day, a snake was next to Anand with its hood up. There are lots of dangerous snakes in Suriname, and dangerous ants. We had seven or eight cows and two coops at home to keep the hens. I took care of all of them, just to make sure there was no dearth of milk, curd and eggs at home. Anand's father used to relish eggs made with fried garlic and onion. He never used to eat rice without homemade ghee.

"Anand used to love dal, curd and ghee and my daughter used to enjoy fresh cream. She used to eat it secretly. When I asked them, they used to tell me, 'The cat has eaten it; we haven't seen it.'

"I used to reply, 'After eating the cream, the cat has covered the vessel with the lid and run away?' Hearing it, they used to run away. Our family has passed through a very tough time. Don't ask me child; don't ask me." Mother looked into Savitri's eyes while completing her sentence.

Savitri wiped mother's body nicely and made her wear a gown and was gently massaging her hands with a little cream. She thought, why should the hands be left out? She applied anti-wrinkle cream on her face, thinking the cream might slow down the process of ageing on her face and her face might glow with the touch of love and affection. As soon as Savitri stopped massaging mother's face, she said, "Look, you make me wear this gown at night at bedtime. I take almost an hour to put it on. I don't understand how to wrap it, where to tie it, where to put my hands." When mother finished her sentence, Savitri bent down slightly and looked into mother's eyes mischievously and mother noticed her straight parting and touched her forehead with her trembling hands and said, "You also do a straight parting like me. Sindoor looks great with such a parting, just as it looks on you. I am not talking about my parting – your parting. Have you seen yourself in the mirror today or not?" Mother was engrossed in the past, thinking about her married life, and it appeared as if she were seeing her face in the mirror with her fascinating eyes and admiring the sindoor in her parting, as if she were feeling proud of her eyes decorated with kajal, her bindi and sindoor.

Before coming out of the bathroom, she said, "Listen, Bacchi, please brush my dentures." Mother removed her artificial teeth and put them in Savitri's hands. Savitri put them in the wash basin and held mother firmly with her hand and made her walk up to the lobby, where Anand was already sitting and waiting for his mother. She made mother sit there and wear a pullover and covered her head with a scarf. Mother wrapped it around her neck with her old trembling hands and tied it with a knot.

"Mother, I will wash your teeth and come back," Savitri told her. She went back to the bathroom, took a bit of Akova white shining cream and started brushing mother's dentures. While brushing she thought that she brushed mother's teeth everyday so that her smile could always shine bright because of it. She also experienced happiness each time mother was happy, and she smiled and laughed that the expression on her face changed and that she forgot her old age. Savitri was very fond of those moments when mother enjoyed herself. That was the reason that she talked about mother's married life. How she wore her nose ring, her bridal attire, lahanga and odhani. Her feet looked attractive with flowery anklets. Her arms were full of bangles and kadas. She also talked about how she sat in the doli and went to her in-laws' place. When mother talked about all these things, her marriage days, one could see a young bride's glow on her face. When Savitri asked her about father, she said she felt shy, as if father at the same age were standing in front of her. He was in the other world. Once, mother said, "My father gave five acres of land, an ox and cows in my marriage. My father-in-law had purchased seven acres of land separately, as one more labourer had come home to sow the crops. Hari Prasad Pandit had arranged my marriage when I was six years old and the Gauna ceremony (a ceremony associated with the consummation of the marriage) was performed when I was twelve years old." After hearing this, Savitri felt that mother had suddenly become a labourer when she was a child. She had never lived the age of adolescence and the pleasure of that age was unknown to her. She had become a mother at the age of eighteen. Anand was still a child and he used to go to the field with his mother, carrying a load on his head.

Mother always used to talk about their work in the fields. "Anand's father used to plough the fields, cut the crops and sow vegetables like Brinjal, bitter gourd, bottle gourd, tomato and various fruits in the fields. He used to pluck the ripe fruit and vegetables in the evening at dusk and store them at home, and at two in the early morning a boat used to sail to Paramaribo from Makhnaita Canal. He used to load all the fruit and vegetables on his cycle and travel a distance of twenty miles, and he reached the place at about four in the morning. Anand also accompanied him. After selling all the produce, they used to return home at about eleven o'clock in the morning. There were no roads at that time, and the money had to be guarded, and riding the cycle was very tiresome. Sometimes father and son used to walk all the way and load all the produce on the cycle.

Our elder son, Anand, had grown up along with many problems. If the cattle did not return till late in the night, he used to go and fetch them. My heart used to sink until he returned. I used to fear that some animal might hit him with its horns. But all our domestic cows and buffaloes loved my son. They used to smell him even in pitch darkness and used to follow him home. Anand knows everything. But he remains silent. He tolerates everything with his silence for my sake." Savitri became sad on hearing this.

Savitri had cleaned mother's dentures and was standing in front of her with them in her hands. She said, "Mama, I have brought dal, rice and lady's finger (okra) for you. I will heat them in the microwave, and your teeth are clean to eat with. Just see, they are shining brightly so that your smile may also shine in the same way." Savitri finished speaking and looked at Anand with a smiling face.

"No, I will not dirty my teeth now. Keep them safe. I'll eat without them," mother said decisively like an order.

Savitri mixed the rice, dal and vegetables and helped mother to eat it with a spoon. Mother enjoyed the flavour. She was not wearing her dentures, as she wanted to taste the food with her gums. The pure ghee seasoning in the dal had filled the taste inside her. Whenever mother was at home with Savitri, she accompanied her into the kitchen. She told her how to cook, how to season the dishes, and she also wanted to taste the aroma. Actually, the people living in the old-age homes in the Netherlands managed to fill their stomachs with boiled food, but neither their minds nor their temptation for tasty food could be satisfied. Savitri was able to realise mother's concern regarding this and hence she normally prepared some Indian recipes and heated them in the microwave so that mother could satisfy herself both with the taste and aroma of the food.

Savitri poured orange juice in a special glass that prevented spilling and placed it in mother's trembling hands. She put a cup of green tea in front of Anand. She made jasmine tea for herself and sat next to mother. Immediately mother said, "Just see, my nails have grown so long. Today, the neighbouring Dutch lady came to drink coffee in the lounge on the ground floor. So, I also went along in my wheelchair. In order to keep my fingers unnoticed by others, I hid both hands in such a manner that people felt that the old lady was sitting like this due to the cold." Mother finished her sentence and looked at Savitri. Tears could be seen in Savitri's eyes. Mother was so concerned about her cleanliness in spite of her helplessness. Savitri had looked at her fingers and nails every day, but she did not find them so long that they needed to be trimmed. Usually, when mother came home once in a fortnight for a few days, Savitri used to massage her hands with mustard oil and also cut the nails and used to store them in a wooden box made of Suriname wood – like her body. Savitri used to keep that small wooden box on a shelf next to her pooja place and used to pray that if God was there then he should protect her mother. She was a mother who had given birth to nine children, had brought them up and now her grandchildren were also becoming old. They also shared their family problems, financial constraints and health problems with the ageing mother and she didn't get a chance to talk about her concerns. She had the biggest concern of the world in front of her, and she could not share it with outsiders, and her own children did not even have the time to listen to her.

Her daughters-in-law were more up to date than the modern women. Her sons worked in the daytime and even cooked food after coming back from work. They took care of the entire household expenditure with their incomes and her daughters-in-law saved their whole incomes in separate bank accounts. If they didn't spend their money for their husbands and children and take care of them, then how could they do anything for their old mother-in-law? If we see it from their point of view, then why should they take care? The old mother was aware of everything, but she kept silent. She knew that her silence was beneficial for herself and her whole family, at least there was scope for meeting one another and maintaining relationships. The old mother's body was free from diabetes and high blood pressure. But her mind was filled with the web of affection for her family and the same warmth was present in her blood. But none of her children had inherited her nature. What is happening these days? One cannot make it out. When the children were small, the mother breastfed them for their growth and when they grew up, she sowed paddy, cut the crops and served them rice for their development. Anand's mother had herself become paddy after working in the paddy fields throughout her life. The quality of paddy that she cultivated in her fields would vanish from the world after her and none of the nations was bothered to get it patented.

Savitri trimmed her nails, but there was no need to cut the nail of her left ring finger, because mother used to tell her that at the time of cutting the crops the nail and the flesh were cut deeply and after that incident her nail never grew again properly. That nail was so soft that mother was able to peel it out with her finger itself.

Savitri managed to store her mother's nails without being noticed by either her mother or Anand. She wanted to place the box on the shelf and started thinking that mother talked in such a balanced way even at the age of eighty-five years and shared her desires and sorrows. If she wanted to eat Indian food, she did not say it directly. She never asked to make Kadi, sewai of kheer. Usually at the time of departure she would say, "Whenever you come here, you cook food and eat the food before coming." She was well aware that if the food was cooked then some delicious food would be packed for her also. When she wanted to get her feet massaged, she would say, "My legs are very painful; I am not able to walk. Look, they have swollen a lot." She said this so that Savitri would apply mustard oil and massage her legs and feet nicely. But she would never ask for it directly. The question of giving an order did not arise at all.

Savitri thought and sat next to her mother-in-law. She looked into the silent and calm eyes of mother and said, "You have so many daughters, daughters-in-law, sons and sons-in-law, grand-children, but we both understand the feelings present within you, just we both." Savitri pointed her finger towards Anand and completed her sentence and looked into mother's eyes with her emotional eyes.

Mother held Savitri's hands with her trembling hands and she opened her heart to Savitri. "Then you take care of me. This is my desire and this is my dream." While saying this, mother looked into Savitri's eyes with her blurred eyes with expectation and started searching for a place for herself in Savitri's response. Before Savitri could say something, mother said,

"Look, my child, when his father was alive, he amassed a lot of wealth and riches. Whether he sold vegetables or fodder, whether cow or ox, whether crops or chicks, he accumulated all the earnings with him. For me he left the money earned from eggs. I used to give that money to my children when they went to school so that they could eat something. Sometimes I used to give them eggs to eat. They used to sell those eggs and eat something of their choice. Once Anand's father sold five or six cows and kept the entire money in the almirah. Anand wet quietly and counted all the money and kept it as it was. He came and told me about it. I know only about those earnings; the rest I do not know anything of. When he left this world, I distributed all the ornaments among my daughters and gave the house and all the land of Suriname to all the sons except Anand. Anand gave all the money for writing the will. He never took a single penny from any one of us. He is a saint. Look, my hands and ears have no sensation. Gold, silver – I do not have anything with me. I have these two hands to bless you, for both of you, and these two ears to hear the sweet voices of all of you." Mother touched her ears while saying this. The holes in her ears were the size of a pearl. Her voice had choked when she spoke the last sentence. Her eyes were filled with tears and her heart was full of love and pain. Their eyes were moist. Their hands were tied due to affection.

The eyes of all three saw the scenes of happiness of love and service and their eyes savoured the flavour of this. Anand's eyes were also wet like his mother's and wife's eyes.

Suddenly a bell rang. A nurse entered the room. She came at nine o'clock at night to check if patient number 515 had slept or not. The nurse was not concerned who the person was or what were their names or religion or even which country or place they belonged to.

Savitri finished her tea. As soon as she moved her hand to pick up the cup, mother said, "Before leaving, make a glass of Bacardi for me. I will drink it after you both leave. I shall sleep happily, otherwise I have to stay awake the whole night." Her tone expressed an order and request at the same time.

Savitri washed the utensils. She mixed some water in her glass and made a drink for mother. She placed a straw in the glass to sip it and kept it in front of mother. She touched her feet and assured her of her presence the next day. Mother blessed both of them with both her hands.

Nobody likes to part like this every day. All of them felt the ache. But they kept quiet and they became sad. Anand and Savitri were disappointed due to their helplessness. They were unable to make room for mother in spite of their willingness, because they were living in a small house. Moreover, the bathroom was upstairs. It was just not just difficult but impossible for mother to climb the stairs and use it.

Savitri wiped her tears inside the closed lift. She did not wipe her tears in front of mother because mother would discover that she was crying. She thought that mother's blurred eyes could not see her tears. But this was only her illusion. Mother's internal eyes could see everything clearly because experienced eyes never become old. In fact, as the experienced eyes grow older and older, everything is seen clearly, even more as they recognise their blood. The nature of blood starts speaking in their trembling hands, so much so that the eyes can even see the future.

GHUTIYA

Suddenly, at two in the morning, the alarm bell began to ring out loud. This caused everyone to wake up. Only the children slept on undisturbed. The people who woke up were internally so afraid and worried that none of them had the courage to get up or to come out of their rooms. Most just buried their faces deeper into their pillows and lay there silently, hoping to go back to sleep as if nothing had happened. Only Ghutiya had the courage to leave her room at once. Three months previously, her eighty-five-year-old mother had arrived from Holland. On her arrival she had managed to break her arm. For several weeks the plaster on her arm caused her a lot of inconvenience. Ghutiya had to look after her alone the whole time. Her daughter-in-law, who was in the Home Ministry, also lived with her and Ghutiya had to look after her needs too as well as bringing up her daughter-in-law's children. There was no question in anyone's mind about the daughter-in-law helping her mother.

Mother's plaster had been removed a week before. Still, she could not sleep at night. She used to spend most of her time lying in bed because of her arm. But suddenly she had come out of her room and entered the drawing room to open the door, hence the alarm going off.

Ghutiya, confused and in panic, came out of her room. She saw her mother sitting next to the door and it struck her that the old lady had hurt herself once more. Luckily, when she went closer, she discovered that nothing was wrong. She was trying to find the bolt at the bottom of the door and was shaking the door. Unfortunately, in this house none of the doors or windows had bolts at the bottom that went into the ground, but mother remembered her old home in Makhainata, where all the doors and windows had bolts at the bottom so she searched for them here too. Her husband had arranged it because she was so short and to be able to open or lock the doors and windows she needed all the bolts and chains to secure the doors and windows to be at the bottom.

Ghutiya herself was already sixty years of age. Only four months before she had had both her eyes operated on. Notwithstanding all of this, there was no way that she could delay her mother's desire to visit Suriname. When her elder brother had phoned to inform her, she had tried to make all kinds of excuses but her elder brother had told her quite frankly, "My mother is like a God to me. By serving my mother I also feel as if I am serving God. Suriname was not just her motherland but also father's Karmbhumi, where he had worked and created his own world. Father is no longer here but his home, house and fields are still there in her memories. She wants to go there. She wants to come with both of us. If we leave it any later, her body will not support her. This I feel will not only be her last journey but a pilgrimage of her soul. We both wish to help her soul make this last pilgrimage. Now you take courage ... just like us."

After hearing this it was impossible for Ghutiya to back out. After getting her mother's arm plastered her brother returned to Holland. To leave his business and live in Suriname for such a long time would create losses. After a few days, Ghutiya found out that her brother's son was going to Holland so she decided to send mother along with him so that she could receive proper care in Farsorking old age home. What would happen if in her old age she broke her hip or suffered a slipped disc? That would create a huge problem! Even at the age of eighty-five, Ghutiya's mother's problem was that she believed that she was no more than forty years old and so she behaved in this manner. She would without any kind of intimation come and go wherever she wanted to. Only yesterday she had taken a plastic bucket and filled it with a little water and one by one put in her feet and spashed the water like a child. Her granddaughter, who had just come home from school, saw her and ran to her mother saying, "Mummy, Mummy, just see what grandma is doing!" If mother was awake, Ghutiya felt that warning bells were always ringing.

After putting mother to bed and making sure she was asleep, Ghutiya managed to sleep for three hours when the sheep's bleating woke her up and she realised that the animal had delivered a lamb. Still, she kept lying on the bed. She had slept at midnight but had been woken up at two o'clock because of mother, and when she slept again, she had no idea. For this reason, her body ached.

In the morning at nine, to get her OAW pension she had to visit the government office to give her doctor all her papers. This would be followed by an inspection of her house by the concerned officers. Ghutiya had never had a job. From the moment she had gained her senses she had been at home looking after her children. From the time she was ten she had looked after her six brothers and sisters. By the time she was twenty she had looked after everyone in her in-laws' house as well as bringing up her three daughters and her only son there too. Now she was looking after their kids too! Not only her son's two boys but her daughter, who, rather than arranging a crèche, left her children with her too when she went to work. For fifty years of her life, she had spent her time in bringing up children. She had found a home neither in her father's house or in her husband's. She had looked after her young brothers and sisters-in-law too when they were children. The fact that she was married was another matter. Now, no one cared about her.

Ghutiya had kept sheep for a long time. Now, after two more were born there were eighteen. She had seventy cocks and hens. Right now, the hens were sitting on fifty eggs and in three weeks, chicks would be hatching. There were forty ducks of whom fifteen were sitting on eggs. As soon as she opened her eyes in the morning, she had to go out to give them food and the day's vegetable and fruit peelings as well as the leftover food she fed them all day long. She let them out of their pens to roam and graze in the five acres next to her house and kept watch over them all day long, gazing at them with her naked eyes or sometimes with binoculars. Whenever the local dogs got into the field, they would catch cocks and ducks in their mouths and later the vultures

89

would join in the feast. So, Ghutiya, through her hard work, had developed quite a profitable farmhouse and managed to support her daughter and son-in-law and their family's needs. In this way, her life was passing her by and she got older. Officials from the pension office used to visit her home from time to time and verify her status, so to protect her two hundred Suriname dollars, she very cleverly hid some of her animals. Others she chased off to distant fields and some she kept in view and explained that they were to be used for her family's food. As the officials left, she presented them with a duck or a cock.

Early in the morning, Ghutiya used to feed the chickens and ducks and manage the lambs. After feeding on the limited food at home she would then open the enclosures and allowed the animals to roam the adjacent field, where they could scratch the earth for food in the green grass. The ducks would swim in the puddles of rainwater and then when they were finished they would come out of the water and start preening and flapping their wings.

Ghutiya till now had looked after her animals with the same love and affection as she had with her children. She kept those sheep about to deliver back in the enclosure and fed them there, whereas she let the other sheep roam in the field and also drove them to find greener grass. In Suriname, after eleven o'clock the sun got so hot she had to take shade under a tree and sit there till five. She could bear the pangs of hunger but not the heat of the sun.

Ghutiya carefully bathed her mother. Whenever she took a bath, mother felt as if she had bathed in the Ganga. Last week, after putting soap and water on this aging eighty-five-year-old body, mother tried to hold onto the tap as she got up. Unfortunately it broke and could not be found. Now they had to buy a new tap to replace it. Until then Ghutiya would have to manage at the main tap outside. She had to check the whole of the house outside so that she could open the main tap and bathe mother.

She gave her mother bread cubes and sugar in hot milk for breakfast. Ghutiya's son, Sandeep, had taken time off to look after mother and his son. Ghutiya had called up her son-in-law, whose office was four kilometres away from Ghutiya's home so that she could go to the pension office. She went to her eldest daughter Rashmi's office with her son-in-law. She went from there with her to the pension office. There was a long line of people waiting to receive their pensions. She took her number and sat down to wait. She thought that the next week she should go to visit the doctor and get papers to ensure a one-year supply of medicines for diabetes, blood pressure and cholesterol. In the Foreign Ministry, her daughter did her best to complete her work. But she could not manage it and sat there frustrated. There was a Surinami lady receptionist. Usually, wherever a Surinami was involved in management they gave preference to their own community. Then they gave preference to the Chinese followed by Indonesians and last of all they gave the Hindustani community a chance.

After finally finishing her work, Rashmi dropped her mother off at the nearest bus station. As some provisions were required at home and milk was required for mother, she went towards the Chinese supermarket. The sun was very hot! In the confusion of finishing her work, she had forgotten to bring her umbrella. Otherwise, usually, just like the sandals on her feet she always carried one in her hands.

After buying the supplies, Ghutiya made her way quickly to the bus station. On the way she stubbed her foot on a stone which she had not seen. She injured her foot and was in pain. Her eyes clouded and she fainted and fell down unconscious. Just then a bus came along and ran over her feet, which caused her a lot of pain and as she began to regain consciousness, a bus came from behind and ran over her chest. The driver, instead of stopping, sped up his bus when he saw the accident and all hopes of saving her vanished.

The milk packet she was taking for her mother fell and burst open. The milk spilled out and mixed with the blood from Ghutiya's body. The right to mother's milk and the debt Ghutiya repaid was in her own blood, in front of all, on the road that afternoon.

Ghutiya used to gulp down milk and water. She also took a long time to drink it. Ghutiya's mother, as well as looking after the children also had to look after the fields and the crops. That is why she called her Ghutiya. But how could she have known that Ghutiya would have to choke down her life as well as being obliged to choke at her death? Not even on the footpath but on the side of the road.

There were no footpaths on the sides of the road in Suriname, even though the coloniser, Ich, had been a Dutch ruler. There he had constructed twenty thousand kilometres of cycle tracks, but in this third-world country he had completely forgotten to make a footpath and provide a drain and sewer line to carry away the dirty wastewater of the houses along the road. The wastewater from bathing and from the kitchens was usually channelled out from behind or in front of the houses through self-dug channels which allowed the wastewater to flow away. It used to mix with the daily rainfall to form large puddles where various kinds of insects like mosquitoes bred quite easily, which the ministry concerned was in no way worried about. Throughout the whole country, public roads were narrow and only for vehicles. As far as pedestrians were concerned, other than in parts of In Paramaribo, the capital, remember there were no footpaths provided for pedestrians on the sides of the roads. Therefore, just like dogs, almost daily people died on the roads. The TV and radio notified people of these accidents. The newspapers too reported these incidents but this had no effect on the government. Ghutiya had written her complaint on the road in blood – at the cost of her life!

BUT PLEASURE!

It was inevitable. The scent of greenery and flowers always reminded her of the luxurious and wealthy game of golf. Lots of people think this is a game only meant for rich and wealthy people. But it is not true. Sheela sometimes wondered why at all she is playing this game. There were continuous requests made by her husband to play and so she involved herself in this game.

But game is the game indeed. She had never been in the mood to read the news which was published in the newspapers or magazines regarding this game. But now she was in the playing field of golf and taking short tips and lessons from her coach. She remembered that when she had to pay fifty Euros to her golf coach it was ridiculous to her. This was an amount which she thought to be very expensive, as in Indian currency, fifty Euros meant two thousand two hundred and fifty rupees. So, she decided not to call her coach the next time and she wouldn't fix any day, time and date for her coach.

During this trial, her husband raised the feelings of domination and jubilation. According to her husband, the game of golf provided company to life and life itself accompanied this game, and afterwards it gave pleasure and solace. Every game has its own tensions and stresses, but in golf this is not needed. Generally, this is the game of friends and is beneficially designed for friends.

In other games there is a continuous demand for fitness and activeness. But in golf this is not needed.

Anyway, Sheela accepted all these pleas and remedies and decided once again to take golf lessons once in fifteen days, and for the rest of the three days in the week, she would practise by herself. One day after covering her ninth hole she said to Rop, her coach, after a fine opening day's display, "I played very good golf today and was under the first nine holes. A bogey on the tenth spilt my calculations, but the birdie on the sixteenth hole helped me level the scores. I will try and play a tighter game tomorrow."

Rob answered, "Well done, Sheela! Now you are improving your game."

Sheela said to Rop, "Sir, will you please excuse me? I have left my purse in the car, and I want to go now."

Rob said, "Okay! I will wait for you in front of the golf office. You can go now." Sheela went out and put her trolley in the car and changed her shoes. Then she started walking towards the golf office. She saw Rob standing there with his girlfriend, Ana. On reaching there, he gave a little introduction. "This is my girlfriend, Ana," Rob said.

"Nice to see you. I am Sheela," Sheela replied.

Sheela saw that the girlfriend, Ana, was seven or eight months pregnant. She gave her congratulations to Ana. "When is this dream expected?" Sheela asked with excitement.

"In two months," Rob answered with excitement and joy. Rob was caressing Ana with one hand and started rubbing gently on her protruding belly, as if he were touching his child.

Sheela said, "Once again, I give you my best wishes, and now I take my leave from your company because my husband is waiting outside in the car."

Both of them said, "Yes, yes; have a nice evening." And then they departed.

Sheela hurriedly went to the lounge. Now, she was not surprised by seeing the bulging bellies of pregnant ladies. There were so many shops specially meant for the clothing of these pregnant ladies. These dresses were specially designed to protect and project the foetus of the pregnant ladies.

In between this, Sheela reached her husband, who was holding a beer glass in one hand and waiting eagerly for her arrival.

Shekhar said with excitement, "Hello, my dear. How was today's play?"

Sheela answered, "Oh! It was fantastic, but today I met the girlfriend of Rop, who is seven or eight months pregnant. They are not married but even then she is pregnant. Okay, it is wonderful."

Shekhar said, "This is not a thing to be surprised about; it is very common in these countries. Before the birth of the child, they must register the name of their partner, and marriage is not a compulsion here. It is only a luxury. By the way, Rob is getting married next week."

"Are we going to the marriage?" Sheela asked.

"You know that here only fifteen or twenty people are invited to the occasion of marriage. The ring ceremony will be held in the city hall and after that a beer-and-wine reception will be organised in a wonderfully decorated hall. I have placed an order with the wine dealer to deliver bottles of champagne to their residence, so they can enjoy the occasion after reaching home." Shekhar said this with ease and in a relieved mood.

Shekhar lived for the happiness of other people and took great care to sustain this happiness. This was his rare quality, which kept him apart from other fellows.

When the waiter arrived, Shekhar ordered beer and a kroket for Sheela. Meanwhile, the friend of Shekhar, who was his golf partner, arrived. They started conversing in Dutch.

While sipping the beer, Sheela started thinking about her visit to Amsterdam. When she had stopped her car before a red light, she had seen a bride and a bridegroom, embellished in the European style. The bride was carrying her fairy-like white satin dress pinched in her hands. Folds of the soft, delicate dress were flowing everywhere. The bridegroom was stepping just behind her and holding the long gown's hem in his hands. He was accompanied by a pair of his friends, who were very close to him. Dusk was just beginning to fall, stifling, in that dim light, the beauty of the bride's prince of love and charm besides crossing the road. While crossing the zebra crossing, her feet were not falling on the road, but she was feeling intensely that they were touching the soft red petals of rose flowers which were scattered beneath her feet. Sheela saw behind the white fairy dress the bulging belly of the bride, who was also seven or eight months pregnant and accompanying her boyfriend, who had now become her husband, with a victorious smile on her face.

In Amsterdam city this scene did not create any miracle for the by-passers going on the roads. This special scene was part of the crowd. But the lover of the bride was looking with intense pleasure towards his girlfriend, who was going to become his wife. Sheela was also spying on the bride, with great pleasure, from inside her car. And she thought that the same scene would happen on the marriage of Ana and her golf coach, Rob. As usual Shekhar was busy talking with his friend. Meanwhile, Sheela started dipping chicken kroket in mustard sauce and putting it in her mouth. While sipping beer she saw Shekhar, who was serious in his discussions. It seems as if something very serious regarding business was fuelling their talk.

Sheela was lost in her reminiscences once again. After the grand reception of her marriage, which was held in the renowned fort of Heemskerk, she went for her honeymoon with Shekhar to Venice. In front of the church, in the famous Marco Square, the newly married couple, with grand paraphernalia, were passing. The bridegroom, who was twenty-five years old, was wearing a dark black suit whereas the bride, who was twenty years old, was in her white fairy-looking dress. They had just accomplished their ring ceremony in the city hall and had come to the world-famous Marco Square.

There were flocks of pigeons flying and gathering at one point – they were the messengers of love. The love couples were chasing and running behind these pure snow-white messengers of love, which symbolised the perfection of true love. It was a warm, glittering sunny day, and light was raining on the earth.

The ramparts were packed with the tourists from all over the world. There was no space left to see their own shadows.

Along the long rectangular field there were the famous branded shops of European goods and materials. The newly wedded couple came to the same restaurant where Sheela was sitting. Fortunately, the singer and pianist and all the musicians were in full flow and mood. The newly married couple were enjoying the joy of their marriage all alone. When the waiter came, they ordered tea. This was a scene of amazement, because they were totally alone but enjoying the thrill, joy and marvellous fragrance of their marriage. The waiter served one pot of tea and two pieces of cookies. The bride offered her piece of cookie to her new husband. The bridegroom, with eyes filled with true love, shared his cookie with his wife.

This was an occasion of celebration. They started dancing with their arms fastened to each other's, their bodies entangled with one another. They started floating on the dancefloor like swans swimming in a pond. They were shaking their legs, and their smiles were knitted with each other's. Their eyes were filled with an intense burning love for one another. This earth was a corner of heaven for them.

The place was overloaded with the presence of visitors, and they found themselves frozen by this miraculous scene. People came and sought their permission to take a few snapshots to immortalise this scene.

They were enjoying these moments all alone, although the place was burdened with so many people. But in fact, there were no friends, no relatives, no near and dear ones with them. They were alone – husband and wife, lover and beloved – but in fact they enjoyed these moments, which fabricated a wonderful world of love. Sheela was peeping in the eyes of everybody and found the same astonished gaze in everyone's eyes. She reinvented the meaning of furtive love with the same frantic devotion that she had once had in her own personal life. The newly wedded couple had restored passion, which was so pressing that they were dying with the intensity of love, kissing each other's lips and sharing these moments of love. Their radiant faces had been turned pinkish-red due to continuous dancing on the floor, but in reality they had returned from the garden of love, which decorated their countenances with an illustrious, mild, delicate, placid fragrance. Sheela also asked their permission to take a few photographs of them. By that time the waiter came and presented the bill. The bridegroom took twenty Euros from his wallet and put them on the plate. Then he caught the hands of his beloved wife and left that place like a victorious Alexander. The victory of love is accomplishment, success, which is true, valuable, more precious than any war victory. Besides your poverty, you will have a dignified feeling of triumph. Ownership of the whole universe will come into your possession. This was the masterfully fabricated scene of love, marriage and life. People were continuously watching the scene until they vanished into the horizon.

Sheela was totally absorbed in the pleasure, which was intoxicating. Suddenly Shekhar came and put his hand on her shoulder. He was talking with his friend at the same time. Sheela reminded Shekhar about going to the mayor's welcome reception party. The time for the party was fixed for between six p.m. and eight p.m. Now they had to freshen up and get ready for the party, so Shekhar went hurriedly towards his car.

They drove at a speed of one hundred to one hundred and twenty miles per hour but it seemed as if the car were just crawling, because of their own anxiety. After reaching their residence they started getting ready for the party very quickly. They very quickly reached the reception hall of the city centre. There was no checking, no police checking, no metal detector. The news was printed in the newspaper that whosoever was willing to meet with the mayor could come and be welcomed by the mayor. The house was open for all and everybody. This was a highly dignified group of people amidst the crowd of ordinary people. Sheela was fascinated by these people. They reached the yard for keeping their overcoats and put their numbers in their coats. A teenage waitress came along with a tray of wine, champagne and juices for serving among the guests. Shekhar and Sheela took their glasses of champagne, said cheers to each other and then stood in the line for shaking hands with the mayor. The city mayor was standing, accompanied by his wife. By his side the national flag was flying.

People were enjoying their drinks of wine and champagne and shaking hands and talking with the feeling of strange thoughts and emotions in the circulatory company of strange faces. Things were progressing in very cool and soothing way, just like the chilled drinks of vanilla ice shakes. They were approaching the mayor, and his royal presence was very thrilling for all the visitors. There were a few people holding flower bouquets. A few were holding costly presents for the mayor. Nobody was in a hurry; things were moving normally.

Sheela saw the mayor's secretary, who was a very good friend of Shekhar, and he had come with his wife to the magnificent marriage of Shekhar He took family dinner at that occasion and sent the wedding photographs by e-mail. While departing from the party he whispered in the ear of Shekhar, "When the intoxication of your honeymoon is finished, check your e-mail in the morning. By the way, this pleasure of the intoxication of the honeymoon will last for so long in the lives of people like you." He said all this in Dutch, and Shekhar had told all this to Sheela in the night.

Secretary Brosman came in front of Sheela touched her cheeks three times and shook hands with Shekhar. He enquired about their welfare. In the beginning there was a feeling of embarrassment whenever the friends of Shekhar touched their cheeks with her cheeks; for her it was ridiculous. When the call bell of her door rang, she never allowed herself to come forward to open the door and entered late in the sitting room. Nobody should reach towards her cheeks. That was the way she shook hands and left the place immediately. But even then she did not escape the tradition of greeting with a kiss. The wives of the friends of Shekhar kissed the cheeks of Shekhar and in return Shekhar also kissed their cheeks. Their husbands marched towards Sheela. This was a courteous way of greeting, engulfed with love and affection, which always filled Sheela with amazement. It was very peculiar that whenever she felt the touch of another man's cheeks on her cheeks, their beard scorched her tender skin, but the beard of Shekhar never pierced her skin in the night. On receiving their greetings and best wishes on the reception of her marriage her cheeks had become dark red because of this.

After meeting with the secretary, Sheela shook hands with the mayor and gave her introduction. Shekhar gave his best wishes to the mayor's wife. They talked about business dealings. The mayor asked Shekhar about his company's card. At that particular moment, the secretary jumped in between them and told the mayor, "I have already got each and every minute detail of their company." They laughed all together at this juncture.

There were two ladies standing on the side of the mayor, supporting him. They were holding beer glasses, their lips wrapped with deep smiles. There was no sign of stress or tension, no proud feeling of standing by the side of the mayor. One of the ladies recognised Shekhar very well. She said something in the ear of Shekhar while touching cheeks in the moments of passing greetings to each other. Shekhar was ashamed of himself and called Sheela to be introduced and invited the lady to their residence. There were official and unofficial photographers talking photographs in different ways. But they were not conscious; no extra pressure of the media was pressing them.

As Shekhar started slipping, holding the hands of Sheela, from that place suddenly Brosman interfered between them said, "Take more drinks after then move." Shekhar met with few more friends. They conversed with each other, got acquainted. They took more wine.

Sheela was wearing a wristwatch, but without looking at the watch she was well aware of the running time. In spite of this, Shekhar was holding her hand as usual. In Europe it is a tradition, holding the hand of a girlfriend, who is generally the wife of that person.

Sheela had the opinion that when she would hold the hand of Shekhar in India, some kind of fuss could be created over there. What bothered her most about that fleeting vision was that she felt it was exactly like her. Something which was natural here was totally unnatural in other countries like Europe. So Sheela always changed the sides of Shekhar while going with him. All this made Shekhar irritated, but he laughed and told Sheela, "Dear, in your country there is a big rush, so we cannot even walk without holding hands, so at least you take good care of me … otherwise I would be lost somewhere."

Shekhar reminded Sheela, "Oh! We have to go to our mother's place ...! She might be waiting for us. Can you imagine our sick mother, lying green and yellow under the powdery light from the window panes? Oh! You know she is perspiring with five o'clock fever, willing to speak to the splendour of the past to her son and daughter-in-law. She shifted just a week before to De Flakhlus old houses. What is a contrast? As she has spent her whole life in a joint family, that is why she is scared being in a lonely room." Sheela thought that this was why her mother-in-law was not taking proper meals, why she was not mixing with anybody. Sheela was flabbergasted to realise the actual condition of her mother-in-law, as she had a heart of soft, mild emotions. Her mother-in-law was of the age of eighty-two years, so she knew it very well. No desire or ambition had survived or been left in the life of her mother-in-law. Sheela recalled that when her mother-in-law was twelve years old, she got married. When she thought to study, she was instead sent to her husband's home (Gauna). Her mother-in-law, who thought to live with ease and comfort, became mother of twelve children. Again, she provided shelter, guidance and support to her children and settled them. They all were settled so well that no space was left for their parents. The father and mother had been broken physically as well as mentally. These were lonely, deserted, discarded creatures, ashamed of their own existence. And the father of the children willingly begged from God never to give him the human life. A few days after, he expired, a sudden death which paralysed the life of the mother.

The mother had acquired a sad, deserted life away from all worldly pleasures. Her husband, on his last time, told her, "You were my life partner for a very long time. You gave support, love, affection, everything, but now I do not want to live any more. This is the time of departure; this is the time to take leave from all contracts life had given to me." So, he staggered and fell down on the bare, cold floor, and a small bottle dropped from his pocket. This was a mystery, because mother was not able to read, so the secret of father's death had remained hidden in the flashes of the future.

In one single day and with a brutal slap, life threw on top of that old lady the whole weight of reality. She shut herself up in her room to weep, indifferent to her children's pleas and explanations as they tried to erase the scars of that misfortune but failed. The husband of that old lady was the centre point of the family. After dusk he used to lock all the eight gates of the house and kept the keys with him. In that gloomy night that poor old fellow, who was familiar with all the locks, had been taken away by the cruel hands of death. Death swept away the life (Pran) from his body, as the eight gates were locked by those same hands. The old lady floundered seeing the sudden death of the father.

For mother, her husband was her life, her ultimate source of energy. Now mother was just spending her days alone, without the presence of the father, in an old age home. The evenings of Shekhar and Sheela were generally going to be spent in the old age home, taking care of their mother, who disliked the tasteless boiled food of the old age home. The expenditure of the old people was being borne by the government, providing three thousand three hundred and fifty Euros per person every month. In spite of this, for a mother who had looked after her twelve children, her corner of the house was her paradise. The mother would never know; she would never be able to shake the fear from her head. She feared to sleep alone in that big old age home, always eagerly waiting to see her son and daughter-in-law. She was always looking towards the road or peeping from the fifth floor of the old age home to recognise Shekhar's car. Otherwise she would sit restlessly in her armchair, her eyes fixed on the gate.

As Shekhar came, he called her with the word "Mumma". She regained consciousness, and her face lightened with a deep smile. Sheela liked her smiles, which showered from her wrinkled face a kind of affection which filled her mind and body. They brought with them a few Indians dishes along with some fruit juices.

For the lady of eighty-two years of age, all of her body was aching. Her neck was also little bit bent.

Sheela asked the mother, "Ma! What have you taken for afternoon lunch?"

Mother gave the reply, "Are kuch na puch ..." (Don't ask anything ...) "Vo hi roj ki nai usnan alu aur poi ki bhazi ... Aur aitat lambka raha ... Hum na zani kaun Ghost raha ... Hum na khaili ..." (It was as usual the vegetable of potato and poi in which was inserted a long, strange piece of something mixed, so she was not able to eat anything.)

Sheela was irritated listening to these things. But she could not say anything except to infuse a new feeling in her. She told her mother-in-law, "Mother, you have to live twenty years more."

"No, don't say such thing," her mother-in-law scolded her.

"Your health is good; you don't have to take medicines. What else do you need?" Sheela said such things in one stroke.

"Na ... Ab hum hiyah na jiyab! Thak gayli hui, bahut bhai!" (No, she didn't want to live any more. She was tired as well as irritated.)

"Kahe?" (Why?) Sheela asked in the same tone as the mother.

"Are, Ab toke ka batai Hua. ekere Bappa hamar bat johat batane. Jab, tab sapna me ave hai. abe kal sapna mai aye rahe to bola raha hum bahut din se bhat na khali hui. Makai ke dana bhuj bhuj ke bhuk katat bati. Hamar shartava bhi bahut din se na dhulal ... Aur aab ka ka batai ...?"

(What should I say? My husband is waiting for me in the heaven. He has nothing to eat, so he is eating baked corn. His shirt is dirty; it has not been washed in a long time. Now what else can I say to you?) She said this and became silent. Tears welled up in the eyes of Sheela. The love, faith and trust for her father, the husband of that old lady, was such wide, long-lasting, real love, which was seen very rarely at this time. That is how people undertake their relations at this time. People are divorcing their life partners. They are maintaining illegal relationships with other men and women. So, when these relations become the symbol of selfishness, this kind of devotion, sacrifice and love is only made in the form of words to be shed from the lips, whereas for the mother of eighty-two years, she wanted to go to the same place where her husband resided, just to serve and fulfill her duties towards him.

Death had squeezed her into life like a spider, biting her in a rage, ready to make her succumb. Her hands were motionless, paralysed by fear, by that irrational terror that comes from within, with no motive, just from knowing that she was abandoned in that old age home. She tried to react but couldn't. Fear had absorbed her completely and remained there, fixed, tenacious, almost corporeal, as if it were some invisible person who had made up her mind not to leave her room. Her crushed and weak body asked nothing. If given something she would eat it, otherwise she would sit idly. In these conditions she was willing to escape from this earth, to prepare the meals for the father (Bappa). The glamour of Europe had not touched her eyes and mind, but the fumes of the chulah (a kind of Indian stove lit by fuel which is made of cow dung) and its firing flames were always roaring in her heart.

This was a heartbreaking incident, so Sheela couldn't talk much more. She was willing to relax her mother-in-law. She wanted to make her cheerful but the idea left her immediately. She then changed the clothes of mother, put a new nightgown on her and took out her dentures for cleaning. She was cleaning the dentures and simultaneously thinking about the mother, who now had no desire to live more, exhausted and tired from the continuity of life.

As usual Shekhar made the mother lay on the bed and kissed her cheeks, telling her to sleep well. Sheela said this to mother just to make her light, "Mama, Hume dar hai Bappa ka sapna dekhne me kahin tum hum sabko chhodke chali na Jayo. Isliaye as sapne me hume dekhna ..." (Sheela asked Mama not to leave them alone when she was busy seeing the dream of the father.)

Sheela was not able to complete her dialogue. Mother interrupted and said, "Bappa jab sapna me na aye hai to munia gay ka sapna dekhila. Badi bhali rahal ... Ek pukar me dhaurat ayat raha. Toke to pura din johve ke padla ..." (Mother said, "When I don't see your Bappa (father) in the dream, I see the dream of

Munia (the name of a cow). She is very good; she runs towards me in only one call, but for you I have to wait for the whole day.) Mama said all this with her full strength as well as transmitting the grief which existed in her heart.

Sheela kissed mother's cheeks, hypnotised by her sweet-smelling eyes. They were soaked with the fragrance of love. Tears dropped over the lips of mother's face.

She said to Sheela, "Roana ... abbe to hum bati ...! Ram Ram bol." (Don't weep ... I am still alive, sitting here ...! Say Ram Ram). Then she took her leave from Sheela. The hearts of Shekhar and Sheela were overloaded with mother's sadness but they could not get rid of this burden.

They reached home, opened the gate of their apartment with the special key and pressed the button of the lift. They met with a Dutch lady, who was residing in the same building, on entering in the lift. "Everything is all right?" As Shekhar asked this question of the lady, she started speaking with them in Dutch.

In her diffused, shaking voice, she started saying, "The day before yesterday Vim had a brain haemorrhage. His whole face and head swelled very badly. I was very scared. Now his left hand and left leg have been paralysed. He cannot see anything; he cannot speak anything. What a calamity has driven over our lives! The blood is spread so thickly in his whole head that the possibility of a CT scan occurs only at the level of zero. When that stops, only then can the treatment be given to him." Yet more shocking statements were to come. She said with benumbed cruelty in her whispering voice, "I told the doctor to give him some medicine which, without any pain, will make him sleep for ever, because I cannot live with this half-dead person. It will destroy my whole life." She completed her whole verdict in one stroke. Sheela was shocked listening to this cruel reality. The news of Vim's brain haemorrhage was not as heartbreaking as the inner feelings of Rit, the Dutch lady, towards her husband. They were so bad and inhumane.

This was not an old story. Last year Vim had celebrated the seventy-fifth birthday of Rit on a very large scale. He made all the necessary arrangements for the party. The place was decked out in finery, coloured paint. Everything was changed. This was a celebration, which was loud, lustrous and one could say directly connected to Vim's heart. He went to everyone's door, knocked and invited them with his whole heart, which was filled with immense pleasure. Sheela had been very happy to see Vim's enthusiasm, so she had gone upstairs and brought her camera from her apartment. She took many photographs of Vim and Rit in different poses, very similar to the photographs of newly wedded people. All the indoor and outdoor work was done by Vim. In this age, Vim was the sole responsible person. He took good care of the indoor and outdoor work. He was the main executive officer, who was in charge of the work from kitchen to garage. He washed the clothes, drove the car. He did all the work. That was the main reason Rit's face always glittered with a shine. The hands of Rit, which were covered with wrinkles, always shone with pink nail paint. Rit was seventy-five years old. Still, before the charm of her smile spread, the colour of her lipstick shone brightly and entered deeply into everyone's eyes. The blooming old age of Rit was totally dependent on the services performed by Vim so perfectly, otherwise she would have been a deserted, crushed, weak old woman living on this earth.

Rit was a totally self-centred woman, who took the pleasures and enjoyments of life only for her own sake. She was not the least concerned with the illness of Vim, but she wished in this situation that Vim should die, because his case was hopeless. She also wondered, if this condition were sustained for a long time, how she would be able to manage all her work, inch by inch, minute by minute, especially with this hopeless case of brain haemorrhage. After all, Vim had not experienced this kind of affliction that his beloved darling wife had deceived him would only serve him for a few days. Throughout his life Vim had loved his wife too much, had taken good care of her, but it was so inhumane that his beloved wife could wish for his death just because he had been paralysed. This kind of selfish feeling towards her husband was a transformation of human beings into mechanical robots, where there was no existence of humanity, a big danger for the whole of society.

In contrast, the mother-in-law of Sheela was a lady, a mother, a wife so whole-heartedly dedicated towards her husband and family only because she loved them so deeply. No shortcut was made for her. The mother-in-law of Sheela was still waiting for the time when she could serve her husband in heaven, wash his shirts, prepare meals for him, no matter whether this could happen in heaven after her death.

So, for two people the meaning of pleasure (Sukh) was totally different. For Rit it was somewhat different. After the paralysing attack on her husband, a beehive had risen up inside the four walls of her skull. It grew larger and larger with successive spirals; it beat on her insides, making the stem of her spinal cord quiver with an irregular vibration.

Her husband was a convenience, a luxury in her life, a path on which she could travel with sophistication. So, when it was needed, she just decided to cut the variable figure from her life, so easily.

She could not understand that someone could have a mouthful of life in abundance but emptiness remained fixed in their stomach, whereas another person, who only had a taste of it, did not want to keep it in their mouth for the next time.

The taste of life and love has different shades. Their meaning varies in two separate ways. Desire and longing to gain worldly pleasures also vary in different directions; to achieve them, everyone has their own ways and values. The method is right or wrong – this is totally dependent on their own moral values.

FÜR AUTOREN A HEART FOR AUTHORS À L'ÉCOUTE DES AUTEURS MIA ΚΑΡΔΙΑ ΓΙΑ ΣΥΓΓΡ
FÖR FÖRFATTARE UN CORAZÓN POR LOS AUTORES YAZARLARIMIZA GÖNÜL VERELIM SZÍ
PER AUTORI ET HJERTE FOR FORFATTERE EEN HART VOOR SCHRIJVERS TEMOS OS AUTO
INKÉRT SERCE DLA AUTORÓW EIN HERZ FÜR AUTOREN A HEART FOR AUTHORS À L'ÉCOU
ÃO ВСЕЙ ДУШОЙ К АВТОРАМ ETT HJÄRTA FÖR FÖRFATTARE À LA ESCUCHA DE LOS AUTOR
ERM KÁ ΓΙΑ ΣΥΓΓΡΑΦΕΙΣ UN CUORE PER AUTORI ET HJERTE FOR FORFATTERE EEN H
ARIMIZA GÖ ERELIM ZÖINKÉRT SERCE DLA AUTORÓW EIN HERZ FÜI
SCHRIJVERS TE CÃO ВСЕЙ ДУШОЙ К АВТОРАМ ETT HJÄRTA FÖ

The author

Professor Pushpita Awasthi was born in 1960 in Kanpur, India. She studied at the prestigious Banaras (Kashi) Hindu University in India and after obtaining her PhD in Hindi literature, Professor Dr Pushpita Awasthi, Indian-origin European woman, flag-bearer of global human sensibilities by embracing language and stimulating literature. Thinker, philosopher, writer, poet, novelist, journalist, activist, associated with many (non)governmental institutions, make her journey diversified, distinct and distinguished.

Her literary journey is anchored in Indian diaspora with many milestone experiences. Her overseas journeys and prolonged stays resonate across colonial cultures and discover pathos, dilemma, deprivation, struggle, identity crisis and loss of culture of five generations trapped in the matrix of origin and adopted country.

She champions global peace, non-violence and humanity in her writings, with relentless optimism that India is poised to dispel the darkness of this materialistic, value-starved world through light of humanity, spirituality, climate concern, nature-centric approach and harmonisation of culture.

The publisher

He who stops getting better stops being good.

This is the motto of novum publishing, and our focus is on finding new manuscripts, publishing them and offering long-term support to the authors.
Our publishing house was founded in 1997, and since then it has become THE expert for new authors and has won numerous awards.

Our editorial team will peruse each manuscript within a few weeks free of charge and without obligation.

You will find more information about
novum publishing and our books on the internet:

w w w . n o v u m - p u b l i s h i n g . c o . u k